To the
Rosete family,
You are no
getting tho

Love,
Kyla

Flashback

Flashback

Kyla LoPresti
1st Edition

This Is A Work of Fiction. Most references to historical people and events are written fictitiously. The use of actual places is not completely accurate and is mainly from the author's imagination.

LCN: 2012908576

ISBN: 978-0-9856078-1-4

Dedication

To my mom and dad for all of their love and support.

Acknowledgements

A special thanks to my reading teacher

Mrs. Dougherty for encouraging me to keep writing.

Also to Richard Krawiec, the first real editor I've ever worked

with.

"Deep into that darkness peering, long I stood there, wondering, fearing, doubting, dreaming dreams no mortal ever dared to dream before."

~Edgar Allan Poe

Prologue: Flashback

My name is *Isabelle Violet Halloway, but* it wasn't always.

My name was *Katherine Elizabeth Jackson,* I was 16 years old.
The year was 1861. I lived with my father and two older
brothers on a small farm in Connecticut. My mother died
shortly after I was born. I had long blonde hair and sapphire
blue eyes. I was an average looking girl. But I knew I was
different, and I knew it in my heart.

Many boys fancied me I'm ashamed to say, but I only
wanted one, and his name was Erik. My father never
approved, so we began to meet secretly. I knew I had a duty
to marry the mayor's son, Nathan Carter, even though I
despised him. But all of that soon changed.

One night my father arranged a dinner with Nathan

and his family to make plans for the wedding. I remember that night very clearly; it was the night I died. I was wearing a sky blue dress (because that was my mother's favorite color) and a corset with a matching sky blue bow to tie back my hair. I had on a diamond necklace and matching earrings. They were my mother's and they were the only expensive things we owned.

It was a cold dark night, unusual for an April evening in Connecticut. My father and I were in a carriage going to meet Nathan to discuss the wedding. I was sick to my stomach thinking about it. Suddenly, the driver stopped. He had hit something. He quickly got up to see what it was. My father and I sat in the carriage waiting for the driver. My father didn't want to get out because his knee was still sore from falling off his horse. But, after the driver didn't come back for five minutes and despite my father's protests I went to see what happened. As soon as I got out of the carriage I was grabbed by someone and a hand was put over my mouth. I knew it was a man because his body towered over mine even with my heeled shoes on. I tried to grab his gloved hand off of my mouth but he held me tightly with his other arm. At first, he didn't do anything, but he squeezed me tighter and tighter mumbling something under his breath.

Maybe goodbye, I thought.

Feeling surreal, my life flashing by, I knew I was going to die. Right then he stabbed me in the heart. The pain was excruciating, but I didn't have the strength to scream. Heaven help me, was it over? In less than a minute my life flashed before my eyes and I was dead. The last thing I saw was a man's face, but it was so dark I couldn't make it out. Now here I am today, every day, wondering what happened in my past.

Flashback

Chapter 1: Reality

As usual I was sitting in my room in Carlsbad, California trying to remember my old life. I missed the laugh of my father, the smiles on my brothers' faces, and the sound of Erik saying I love you. I always loved going to bed. I could actually be back in my old life. Although, I never remember everything, bits and pieces aren't always there. However, when I wake up reality sets in and I realize that I can never go back. This is reality now, and I have a new family. I don't have a guy that I'm deeply in love with. I don't have two brothers that always protected me. I do have an obnoxious older sister and I actually know my mom in this life. Not all of my dreams remind me of my past. Some of them take place in the future and I can see bad things that might happen. My life is confusing, and I feel like I am in it alone.

Flashback

Just as I was about to close my eyes my older sister banged on my bedroom door. My sister's name is Jocelyn. She has shoulder length blonde hair and brown eyes. She is tall, skinny, and pretty. I think we resemble each other. In this life I have straight brown hair and hazel eyes with flecks of gold in them. I'm tall and skinny too, and I guess I'm pretty.

"Iz," Jocelyn shouted from the hall, still banging on the door, "I need to talk to you."

"Come in," I yelled back.

"What's wrong? You look like you've seen a ghost."

There she goes again, acting like she's a concerned parent. I mean honestly; she's freakin' 19 years old. I'm not that much younger than she, I'm sixteen, not a child. "I'm fine," I said.

"Are you sure? You look pale and upset or something," she said. "You know you can tell me anything."

But that's just it, I can't tell her, or anyone. Not even my best friends. I mean really, what am I going to tell them? That I'm freakin' reincarnated? That I was from the 1800's and was murdered by God knows who? They'll think I'm a damn nutcase! I am not a nutcase! Am I?

"Yes," I yelled, sounding annoyed.

"Forget it," she said, "Just know that I'll always be there for you when you need me."

Flashback

"Whatever," I muttered.

And with that, she left, leaving me with not knowing what she wanted. I rolled over and tried to fall asleep. I scanned my blue walls, looking at every picture that hung on them. I couldn't go to sleep. I kept trying to compare my old bedroom to this one, but I was having a hard time remembering. Is this how it's always going to be? I may never remember everything about my old life, especially since I can't even remember my bedroom. I faded off to sleep, hoping to have a good dream.

Chapter 2: Store

The music blared in my ears; the smell of overly priced cologne and perfume irritated my nose as I pushed aside some hangers on a sales rack. I was shopping for clothes at Hollister with Evelyn and Rachael. I felt a presence. It was almost like there was a ghost there and I had the strangest feeling that I was being watched. I continued to look through the skirts anyway. I was totally ticked that they didn't have my size in the blue skirt, so I had to go with the white. Like I need any more clothes?

"Hey Ev, you find that pink sweatshirt yet?" Rachael called from where she was standing, of course, right by the yoga pants. She desperately wanted those yoga pants, but she only had enough money for a belt.

"Nope, I'll have to try at the outlets. Ooh we should

Flashback

go to Victoria's Secret next, they have lots of yoga pants," Evelyn joked.

I laughed.

"Not funny you guys," She said clutching a pair of sky blue yoga pants in her hands.

That made me laugh even more.

We got in line getting ready to check out. I felt a cold burst of air against my neck. I tensed up.

"Did you guys feel that?" I asked hoping that I wasn't delusional.

"What are you talking about?" Evelyn asked.

I quickly turned and saw someone vaguely familiar exiting the store.

"Just forget it," I said to them, "I'm just a freak," I muttered to myself. I wanted to run out of the store, but I had to pay for my stuff first. Then, I walked up to the cash register. Of course it wasn't a cute guy; it was an annoying preppy blonde girl.

"How are you doing today?" She asked in some kind of fake Jersey girl accent.

Rachael rolled her eyes and Evelyn put her hand over her mouth trying not to laugh.

I didn't mean to, but I looked her up and down. She had on some weird, flowy, black blouse and purple skinny jeans. She looked like she just hopped out the 1980s. No, she looked like she could be Justin Bieber's twin. I held back a laugh, "I'm great, how are you?" I think I mimicked her accent.

"Is this it for today? We have a huge sale on yoga pants. Buy two get one half off."

My friends and I started cracking up. Yeah huge sale. Their yoga pants are like forty dollars each.

The preppy girl gave us a look like we were total weirdoes. Yeah, we're weirdoes; did she look in the mirror before she left her house?

"Yeah, that's all," I said handing her the skirt and a tank top.

"That will be $70.17."

"Okay," I said as I rummaged through my purse looking for my debit card.

She swiped my card and handed it back along with the receipt.

"Thank you," I said picking up my bag.

"You're welcome, have a nice day!" She said in her fake accent.

Jeez she's annoying. I waited for Evelyn and Rachael to check out. When they were done, we left and walked to Rachael's car. I felt like someone was following me again. A fancy silver car sped by us as we got into the car.

Chapter 3: School

I was standing outside my house waiting for Rachael to pick me up for school. I was wondering why I dreamt about the day we went shopping at Hollister last week. I didn't recall any of my other dreams from the night before especially, not ones about my past.

She was taking forever. When was I going to get my own car?

Finally, she pulled up to my driveway in her red mustang convertible. Rachael's long, dirty blonde hair was moving in the wind. Her dark brown eyes contrasted against her pale skin. As I made my way to the car I could smell her cherry lip gloss, and hear her singing "What the Hell" along to the radio. Just what I was thinking, what the hell was she doing? Trying to wake up the whole neighborhood?

"Hey," Rachael said.

"Hi," I said back, getting in the car.

"Guess what," she said.

"What?"

"I heard this really hot new guy from Italy or someplace, I don't know, transferred to our school."

Rachael and her freakin' rumors. "Cool."

"I heard he's like really smart and speaks like five languages."

I don't know where Rachael gets all her info about people, but she seems to know everything about everyone. "Where did you hear that?"

"Well, London's aunt works in the school office and she saw the hottie's transcripts."

"I can't wait to meet him." Not. Like he will ever talk to me if he's as hot as Rachael says.

As soon as we got to the school I saw Evelyn waiting by the front gate for us like always. We can't miss her. Evelyn likes to stand out, and in her shiny silver shirt and short jean skirt, she stood out today. Evelyn has dyed blonde hair and hazel eyes, but her natural hair color is strawberry blonde. She's short, skinny, and always tan. I think she bleaches her teeth, but won't admit it. But when she smiles she looks like she has a mouthful of Chiclets.

"Hello," Evelyn said.

"Hi," Rachael and I said in unison.

Rachael and Evelyn started a conversation, but I wasn't really paying attention, trying to make sense of my dream. I think it was about the new kid. So I guess it was true.

*

The rest of the morning blew by quickly, and before I knew it, it was lunchtime. None of us ever buy lunch because it is so gross. So, we usually brown bag it and we all share. We spread our snacks out on the table. I, of course, had Smartfood, Ev had some kind of homemade muffin her mom baked and Rachael put down some chocolate bars. I was psyched that she brought chocolate because I was totally craving it. I was munching on my candy while Rachael and Evelyn were fighting over which band was better, Coldplay or Never Shout Never. That's when I saw him.

Could it really be him? It was Erik. I knew it. I could hear Rachael and Evelyn saying my name, but I wasn't

Flashback

listening to them. My body was numb and I couldn't stop staring; I had a million questions in my head. How was he here? How was he still alive?

Just then I got snapped out of my thoughts, they were shaking me.

"What?" I said, obviously annoyed.

"Are you ok?" Evelyn asked.

"I wish people would stop asking me that!" I snapped.

He looked at me when I yelled, his eyes sparkling. He looked at me intently, but quickly looked away.

"Fine," Rachael snapped back.

"Look, I'm sorry," I said, "I guess I'm just tired." I was tired. I hadn't been sleeping well lately. I was nervous and I didn't know why. I couldn't remember a lot of my dreams. And now I thought Erik was here.

"It's fine," Evelyn said, "Ohhhh, and by the way, hot new guy's staring at you."

"Yeah," I muttered, "Probably because I'm a total nutcase."

"No, because you're beautiful," Evelyn said, "Now go out there and win his heart."

"Do I have to?" I really didn't want to face Erik, if it was really even him. Why does my life have to be so confusing? Am I the only teenager in the world that weird stuff happens to?

"Yes you have to talk to him, he keeps checking you out," Rachael said pushing me out of the blue metal chair I was sitting in, "Now go."

Chapter 4: Confrontation

I didn't want to do this, at least not now. But I had to. Wait, no I didn't, what the frigg was I thinking. But it was already too late; I was already in front of him and nervously blurted out the word "hi" before I could think. My hands shook and my voice quivered. His piercing green eyes brightened at the sound of my voice.

" Hello," he said his eyes boring into mine. He looked just like Erik, could it really be him? My eyes uncontrollably scanned his flawless body. He was perfect, just like Erik. He didn't have a piece of hair out of place and his clothes looked perfectly tailored.

"Well, well, well, look what we have here," said London from behind me, interrupting us.

Of course it was London. She's the most popular (and bitchiest) girl in school. But I wouldn't call her well liked or a role model. Her hair and make-up is always impeccable and she wears the nicest clothes. She also drives a Porsche. I don't even know why she goes to our school, other than to make my life miserable. Her parents have enough money to send her to a boarding school in England or something. I really don't know what they are waiting for.

Laughing she said, "What's wrong loser? Get lost from your nerd herd again? Because you certainly don't look like you belong with the new guy."

"No, actually I didn't, why are you bothering me? Don't have a life of your own, I see. Oh and loser? Really? Couldn't come up with anything better?"

She just stood there gaping at me. God, it felt good to tell her off for once. Was this the new me? I had a weird burst of nerve. "Exactly what I thought," I said turning away and leaving the cafeteria, forgetting all about the new kid. Yeah, he was totally going to talk to me now. Not.

*

As it turned out I had two classes with *him*. English second period and Drama Club at the end of the day. I didn't acknowledge *him* in English class because I didn't know what to say, but he stared at me all through Drama. It was so embarrassing when our drama teacher, Ms. Gale, asked me to sing. I'm good at singing, but it felt weird with him there. All he did was gawk at me, emotionless. No matter where I moved his eyes were always on me.

After school was over I rushed to Rachael's car not wanting to talk because I was too nervous. I sensed him behind me and I knew for sure it was in fact Erik. As soon as I opened the car door, he pushed it closed with his hand. I looked up at him and said, "What?"

I could tell he knew I was pissed off. With his hand still on the door, and his eyes once again, boring into mine he said, "Do you know who I am?"

Of course I knew who he was! Was that a trick question? "Yes," I said, "Now can I get in the damn car?

Ignoring my question he said, "No, really, do you know who I am?"

"Now let me answer that question with a question," I said. "Do you know who I am?"

Sighing he said, "Yes, Isabelle."

"Then who?" I asked with a smile.

I was really trying his patience now. But I didn't care. It was actually quite funny. We used to play back and forth like this when I was with him. I was so anxious; I couldn't believe it was really happening.

"How can I know it's you, my love?"

"Just like I know it's you," I said matter-of-factly.

He started to say something, but I cut him off. "How are you still alive?" I blurted out nervously.
But as soon as I realized what I said, I felt awkward and unsure if I should have asked him.

"It is you," he whispered, making me tingle all over. I was starting to feel lightheaded and apprehensive.

"Ummm... I got to go." I started to open the car door. I really didn't want to start this now in front of Rachael and I was afraid to learn the truth. My mom was waiting for me to get home anyway so we could go to the mall. Maybe doing a little shopping would clear my head.

Rachael started the car.

"Wait, do you want to go to the beach with me on Saturday? I could explain."

"Yes sounds good, pick me up at two," I said, and turned and got in the car. I needed some time to comprehend this. If he was reincarnated like me, how could he still look

the same? Am I nuts? Was someone playing a joke on me? I
wanted to throw up.

Chapter 5: Conversation with Rachael

"**What** the hell was that?" Rachael questioned as soon as I got in the car. This was going to be a long car ride home.

"Nothing." I muttered. My stomach was still sick.

"Yes that was something!" she said. "Now spill or I'll make your life miserable."

"Already accomplished that," I said in the snotty tone I sometimes get when I am annoyed with my friends.

"Whatever." She said rolling her eyes at me. "Now tell me!"

I thought about telling her now just to get her to shut up, but I decided to wait. Making her crazy was fun. "Not right now, let's just listen to music," I said.

"Uh – fine," she sighed, "But as soon as we get to your house, you're spilling."

The rest of the ride home was silent, never thought I'd

Flashback

see the day. As soon as we were in my room, she starting asking me all these questions. I only told her that he asked me out.

"We just talked," I answered.

"No way, about what, what else happened…" she rambled on. "How do you explain the way he looked at you and why he was so close to you? You better hurry up and tell me before your mother gets home."

"You didn't let me finish," I said.

"Go ahead, continue," she shrugged, mimicking me.

"And, we're kind of going on a date on Saturday."

"Kind of!" She said as she raised her eyebrows. "No one kind of goes on a date. Did he ask you out or not? And where are you going?"

"The beach." I answered. I was reluctant to give her any more details.

"Great!" She exclaimed.

Exactly, great. She was getting all perky again. It is hard to keep things from Rachael when she gets all excited about the things I tell her. She has a way about her that gets people to tell her intimate details about their lives. Like the time I told her about t how I kissed her cousin Shane last year after I promised him I wouldn't. I knew I'd better wrap it up or I would end up telling her my whole life story. Then, she would really think I was crazy.

"So he'll get to see you in your bathing suit," she said. "You are wearing your bathing suit, right?"

I shrugged, "I'm not sure, I was thinking about just wearing shorts and a tank top.

"You have got to be kidding me! You're wearing a bathing suit, at least under your clothes."

"Fine," I said under my breath. I started to daydream and wondered how Rachael would be when she plans her wedding one-day. I would love to be a fly on a wall on and watch her. She would never be able to pick out a dress or flowers, or even a groom for that matter. If she had a groom she would probably cancel the wedding the day before anyway.

"Oh, and imagine what you will talk about with him." She looked revolted at the thought of me actually having a conversation with a boy. "I am going to have to get you an earpiece and tell you what to say! Or I should give you notes about what to talk about and you can study them. Yup, that's a great idea, I am a genius."

Great! As if I didn't have enough stuff to study already. She's probably gonna want to teach me how to properly apply mascara, too. She droned on and on about getting me ready for my date but I really wasn't paying attention. I was thinking about Erik.

Flashback

Chapter 6: Shopping With Mom

We pulled up to the strip mall and my mom parked her white Highlander right in front of the Coach store. My mom really wanted a new pocketbook for their anniversary, which was like a month away. She was totally showing me the one she wanted so I would tell my dad. After that we went to the food court. I was so in the mood for some Wetzel's Pretzels. I ended up getting the cinnamon and sugar pretzel with water, but my mom just got the salted pretzel with lemonade. We went to sit down at the small metal table to eat when my mom saw her friend.

"Emily?" A woman asked.

"Angela? Oh my gosh it is you!" My mother said gasping.

What's the big deal with this short, red headed lady? She reminded me of someone I once knew, she seemed very kind. The lady, Angela, ran up to my mother and hugged her.

Flashback

"How are you? Oh and is this your daughter? Isn't she beautiful! Is this Jocelyn or Isabelle?"

"This is Isabelle; Jocelyn is with her father looking at UCLA and Berkley today. Where is your daughter?"

"She's coming right now," Angela said turning around.

Oh my God. It was London Carter, coming up with her bright red lipstick on, and jet black hair. She had a bunch of bags, like five in each hand. All from Armani, Guess and Coach, should I go on?

"Ma, who is this?" She asked in her snotty attitude. She knew exactly who I was, but refused to look at me.

"This is Emily and Isabelle Halloway, Emily's an old friend of mine. We go way back. Do you know my daughter Isabelle?"

"Yeah, of course I do, she practically introduced me to the new guy Erik at our school," I said to spite her.

She looked at me in disgust. I smirked.

"That's nice London," her mother praised her.

She obviously didn't see Satan right behind those innocent looking blue eyes of hers.

"Thank you mother."

"I bet you two are great friends in school."

"Totally! We text like all the time," London lied.

What? I don't even know her number. I can't believe

she was playing into my story. My line totally backfired.

"Well, we have to get going," Angela said, "We'll have to plan to hang out, just the four of us. I'm sure the girls will have a great time."

Highly doubtful.

"Sure, just call me and we'll make plans."

"All right bye," Angela said.

"Bye Isabelle," London whispered in my ear as she walked by me swinging her bags on her arm.

"Well wasn't that fun?" my mom asked, "They are very nice people."

I just nodded. My mom is so naïve sometimes.

After we ate our pretzels we went to Deb. I got this cute tank top and shorts to wear to the beach Saturday. The tank top was a pretty hot pink spaghetti strapped, and the shorts were denim. I also got this totally hot teal bikini to wear just like Rachael said I should. We went into a couple of other stores I like, but I felt bad making my mom spend any more money so I didn't get anything else.

When we got home at 8:00 I was beat, partially from all the walking, but mostly from seeing London. She just sucked the life out of you every time you went near her.

Chapter 7: Rewind

It was March 4, 1861. Abraham Lincoln had just been elected the President of the United States. There was a party at the Mayor's mansion to celebrate his election. I was in my room brushing my hair, getting ready for the ball. I was wearing an emerald green satin dress and corset. I wore my wavy blonde hair down and I had a diamond hair clip on that was my mother's. I did not want to go to the ball, but my older brothers' James and Daniel insisted I go. They wanted me to meet a friend. The nerve of those two, they knew I did not like the Mayor's son. Even my father was adamant that I go. He said Nathan fancied me, and it would be a good idea to get to know him better. But, I knew enough about him to know I already didn't like him. Nathan was a pig. I couldn't believe my father wanted me to marry him!

Deep in thought, I lost track of time. It was already time to go. My brother James opened my door.

Flashback

"Katherine, time to go!" He said making me jump.

"You could have knocked you know."

"I did several times."

"Oh, I didn't hear you. I was day dreaming."

"Probably dreaming about Nathan and how much you love him. Oh, I know you want to kiss him," he teased.

"Do not." Gross, I was completely revolted at the thought.

"Do too."

"No."

"Sure you do!"

"James, do not bother the girl," Daniel said, coming in my room.

That was just like Daniel, breaking up our fun. Always being so serious, treating us like kids. James and Daniel are twins and yet they are complete opposites. They have the same sandy blonde hair and blue eyes, but their personalities are totally different. James is fun, enthusiastic, and loud. Daniel is serious, quiet, and very intelligent. I guess Daniel can be fun when he wants. He was more like James when we were younger. They are both warm-hearted and always look out for me. They're my shoulders to cry on, my protectors, and my life. I didn't want to think about leaving my home with them to marry Nathan.

"Daniel, don't get your knickers in a bunch. I was just kidding." James snapped.

"Yeah, we were just..."

"Kat, don't speak. I saw what happened," Daniel said cutting me off.

"Don't mind him, father yelled at him for reading too much," chuckled James.

"Children," Daniel muttered and left.

"Let's go," James said, "If we don't hurry Mr. Sourpuss will leave without us."

I laughed at that.

When we got outside there was a carriage waiting for us. I got in and realized that father wasn't there.

"Father's not coming?" I asked no one in particular.

No," Daniel said as the carriage pulled away from our house.

"Why?"

Daniel didn't answer.

"Daniel, answer me!"

"Why is it so important to you anyway?" He snarled.

"Because I want him there. I don't know why you are so offended about it." I snapped back.

I hate it when we fight. We almost never do. Daniel is

Flashback

never like this. Daniel is so quiet and not argumentative. He has always taken care of me since mother passed away.

Something was upsetting him and making him on edge.

"Kay," James said sighing, "Dad's courting someone." Of course Daniel was upset about this. He actually remembered our mother. I was just a baby when she died. He and James were four. He has always told father that nobody could replace her. He was probably afraid that this woman would.

"Who?" I was intrigued.

Father hasn't courted anyone since our mother died.

"That new lady in town, Anna," Daniel said with disgust.

Anna was a small-framed woman with long, straight, red hair and warm green eyes. I didn't know how Daniel could dislike her. She was a kind woman.

"Oh..." Daniel started to say something but we had reached the ball and had to get out of the carriage. The driver let us out and showed us to the entrance. We walked into the Mayor's mansion. There were so many people but of course I saw Nathan first, and he spotted me immediately. His greasy black hair was shining in the lights of the chandelier in the grand ballroom. His tailcoat was so long I thought it was hitting the floor as he walked towards me. He ran up to me and pulled me into the crowd. Everyone from the town was at the ball. He pushed through people as if he was the head of the town. He led me to a balcony that was up a large winding staircase in the back of the room, where he knew we would be all alone. The balcony overlooked a beautiful garden. The moon was so bright, it illuminated all of the flowers. I could have all this, I thought. However, I would be miserable and it was not worth it. I needed to figure out a way to not marry Nathan.

"Where have you been hiding?" He slurred.

He was so obviously intoxicated. "I...I just got here," I stammered.

"Sure you did," his hot breath was in my face.

"I really did," I said trying not to make him angry.

"Stop lying, you know what, let's enjoy this," he garbled. He pulled me close to him squeezing my butt and trying to kiss me. His hot breath tasted horrible.

"Get off of me!" I screamed trying to pull away.

"Come on my sweet, don't be like that," he said still gripping me tightly.

"She said get off of her!" A voice came out of nowhere. Thank you God, someone was here to save me from this wretched guy.

Flashback

"Mind your own business," Nathan slurred, which came out like miyoronbiznus.

"I guess I wasn't clear. I said get off of her."

"Darling you really don't want to do this," Nathan said to me pushing closer to the edge of the balcony.

"And why is that?" I said flatly.

"Because, my father can ruin you," Nathan spat.

"Is that a threat?"

"It could be."

"Just shut up and get away from her, and that is a threat," the man shouted.

"Alright, alright, take it easy," Nathan said backing away.

I thought he was going to leave, but suddenly he turned back around and pinned me against the wall and then let me go. He muttered, "This isn't over." I fell to the ground sobbing.

"Are you okay?" The man asked, leaning over me.

I just sat there for a minute looking him up and down. The first thing I noticed was his piercing green eyes and his mesmerizing smile.

He had wavy brown hair and a muscled body. He wasn't dressed as well as the other men at the ball but that didn't matter. He was handsome and I am sure girls fawned all over him.

"Yes, that's normal for Nathan."

"Do you put up with him all the time?" He asked helping me to my feet.

"Unfortunately, I have to."

"Why?"

"It is what my father wishes," I said trying not to cry again.

"It should not matter what he wishes, you would like to be happy wouldn't you?"

"Yes," I mumbled.

"Speak up!"

I was definitely not going to take advice from a man I didn't even know. It is my life and I can figure it out on my own.

"Please excuse me, I need to go, my brothers are waiting for me. It was..." I stopped trying to think of a word, so I just went with "nice meeting you."

I ran down the stairs, not wanting to talk to him anymore.

"Wait," he called after me. I didn't turn around. I felt like such a fool I didn't want to see him ever again. I kept running and didn't see where I was going. I bumped into someone, and when I looked up I saw that it was James.

"Katherine, where have you been?"

I didn't have to answer that. As soon as he realized my face was all puffed up and red he knew I had been crying.

"Nathan," he hissed and pulled me into a hug. "It will be alright, I won't let him hurt you."

He pulled me out to face him, "I almost forgot we want you to meet someone, Daniel is getting him."

"Who?"

"Good, your face isn't puffy anymore."

"I love how you keep things from me," I teased.

"I have to," he said under his breath.

I wasn't sure if I was supposed to hear that, but I did. I wasn't sure what that meant. I didn't get a chance to respond because we were interrupted.

"Great, Daniel, you brought him!"

I didn't need to turn around to know it was him. I gave James my 'seriously' look and he gave me his 'what did I do?' look.

"Katherine, please turn around," Daniel sighed.

I looked at James for help but he just shook his head yes. I turned around and I couldn't help but look right into those beautiful eyes. His rosy lips were curled up in an awkward smile. I couldn't get over how wonderfully charming he looked. I could see how a girl could easily fall in love with him. But I didn't. My annoyance with him out-weighed his good looks.

"Katherine, this is our friend Erik," Daniel said brightening up at the thought.

I was glad that Daniel had a friend, and he seemed to make him happy. But did it really have to be Erik, the guy who just saved me from Nathan? The one I looked like a fool in front of. James nudged me to say hello.

"Hello," I said as I curtseyed.

He chuckled, "And hello to you again. Would you like to dance? It is a ball after all."

I looked at my brothers to get me out of this situation. Instead they nodded to me with encouragement. I gulped and put my hand out for Erik to lead me onto the dance floor.

As soon as we started dancing Erik said, "I'm sorry."

"What?"

"I am sorry for yelling at you about your life. I don't even know you." He took the words right out of my mouth.

"It's fine," I said smiling. I was starting to really like this Erik guy.

"Good, I'm glad. I wouldn't want you mad at me."

He started twirling me around. As we danced it felt like the dance floor was ours, and we were the only people in the world. He pulled me close to him and I laid my head on his chest. The dance was over and everyone began to clap. I didn't notice that everyone parted to watch us dance and we were really the only ones on the dance floor. I saw Nathan in the far corner. His face was beet red and he looked furious. Just to spite him (and because I really like Erik) I kissed him on the cheek.

Chapter 8: One Day Until The Big Date

My phone vibrated on my night stand. I turned over and picked it up. It's 5:45 am. I was just having a wonderful dream about the day I met Erik. Why in the world is Rachael texting me so freakin' early?

I'm not going to school. I 'm sick ☹ her text said.

Great, now I have to text Evelyn and see if her mom can bring us in the minivan.

Ev, can you take me to school Rach is sick

Sure. She texted back.

I fell back to sleep for what seemed like five minutes when my alarm clock started playing the song of the day, *Your Love Is My Drug* by Ke$ha.

I was getting really sick of the song.

I rolled out of bed and started rummaging through my

Flashback

drawers for my black lace tank top and cardigan. I put on some Aeropostale jeans. I went to the bathroom and scrunched my hair, because I really wanted to see how my hair looked that way. Most of the girls do it, so I tried it out. It actually looked pretty. I put my music note necklace on and did my makeup.

I ran downstairs. My parents were at the table eating breakfast.

"Do you want something to eat before school?" My mom asked.

"No thanks, ma." I said from the living room.

"Okay, your lunch is on the counter." Yeah, my mom still packs my lunch for me. What can I say? She knows what I like and she makes it better than I do.

I had left all my books and folders on the end table so I had to grab everything quickly before Evelyn came. I threw everything in my bag and ran into the kitchen to get my lunch. "See ya later," I said to my parents.

I waited for like a minute before Evelyn's mom pulled up in my driveway. She's the type of lady who's never late no matter where she's going. She always has to leave her house like ten minutes early. She opened her minivan's door with one button, and I hopped in. No, not like a rabbit.

Flashback

"Hey Iz," Evelyn said.

"How are you Isabelle?" Mrs. Moore asked. "Would you like a cookie?" She asked shoving a bag of cookies in my face.

"Whoa, mom, put the cookies down and drive," Ev said waving her hands down.

Evelyn mouthed sorry to me. She looked embarrassed.

'It's okay,' I mouthed back shrugging.

Evelyn's mom is like Martha Stewart, she's constantly baking. Once she made this crazy duck sculpture out of fruit. It was insanely good. I swear she should have her own cooking show. I bet she would love redecorating her kitchen for every show. Maybe I could guest star?! That would be fun. I'd like to see that happen. Even Rachael could help with the show. She could give her fashion tips and help decorate the kitchen. I laughed silently to myself.

Her mom pulled up right in front of the school. Like riding in a minivan wasn't torture enough. And to top that, she had little stick figures of her family on her trunk. The whole school could see us.

"Bye, mom."

"Bye, Mrs. Moore," I said getting out of the car trying to not be seen.

"Bye, girls, have a nice day," she practically shouted out of her window. Does she need a bullhorn to announce it to the world? A bunch of kids looked at us weird. Evelyn gave them dirty looks and they backed off.

"Could my mom be any more embarrassing?" She asked as we walked to our lockers.

"Believe me, you got it good. Yesterday I had to spend twenty minutes talking to the devil's spawn and her angel like mother. My mom was practically all over her mother, 'Oh, Angela could it be you' 'Yes Emily, it is. How are you and your beautiful children?" I mimicked my mother and Angela.

Evelyn laughed, "What did London say?"

"She pretended not to know me until I told her mother that she practically introduced me to Erik. She got so pissed, and pretended we were such great friends, and that we text all the time."

"Rough,"

"Tell me about it."

"Speak of the devil," Evelyn said.

I slammed my locker shut and turned as London walked by. She looked at us fiercely, flipped her hair, and walked away.

"Brat," Evelyn muttered. That's her code word for... It's not that hard to decipher.

"Let's get to class," I said as the bell rang. We skipped homeroom.

Evelyn and I walked to math class.

My math teacher, Mr. Simmons, was droning on and on about some kind of Trigonometry. I wasn't really paying attention; I was wondering what Erik was going to say to me tomorrow. My hands were scribbling bare trees with some sort of light coming out of it on a piece of paper.

"Miss Halloway," Mr. Simmons said coming up to my desk and looking down at my drawing. "Would you like to share what you have drawn with the class?"

I heard a bunch of people laugh.

"No sir." Thank god he really didn't want me to show my drawing. It looked like a five year old did it.

"I thought not, now start paying attention, please."

Uhhh, did he really have to stick me out like that? As if people don't think I'm a freak already. "Okay," I said softly, trying not to get embarrassed.

I saw Evelyn shrug out of the corner of my eye.

*

I walked to English alone because Evelyn had to go to the principal's office for some reason. I strolled in and I saw Erik sitting at a desk. I went over and sat down next to him. He smiled at me, "Hi."

"Hi," I said smiling back.

Mrs. Harris came in and started talking about Charles Dickens. But I already knew enough about him from Daniel. I could probably teach her some things.

Erik laughed. I didn't know what was so funny.

"The book, *Oliver Twist*, is about child labor. That was very common in the 1800s."

Okay, I do not need a history lesson about my past. My father never had us work like those people in the book made those children work. I really didn't want to hear about Poor laws or any other laws from back then, since I didn't agree with most of them.

Erik laughed again. Oh, my God! What the hell was so funny?

Mrs. Harris continued to talk about how the town Oliver was born in was unnamed, but I know that in the original writings the town was called Mudfog. I remembered that clearly because I once had a dream about Daniel laughing about the name.

Erik kept looking at me as the teacher spoke. Maybe

because he remembered the same stuff about the novel as I did.

Mrs. Harris went over our assignment for the book. She wanted us to research Charles Dickens and why he wrote about an orphaned boy. As she spoke I tried to remember all the things Daniel had told me about him. I really did not want to have to do any research if I could recall some important information. I jotted down some facts. I knew that Dickens himself was a child laborer in his youth and maybe that's why he wrote a book about it.

Erik was watching me write frantically as I began to remember more and more. He smirked. I rolled my eyes at him and kept writing. Charles Dickens really wanted his readers to question the social injustice that was going on in London at that time. I knew this had upset Daniel when he read about it back then. I started to tear up a little when I thought about Daniel.

The bell sounded and it was time to switch classes.

Third and fourth period ended quickly. Then it was lunch. Rachael wasn't there so it was just Evelyn and me. Evelyn had some of those homemade chocolate chip cookies her mom made, and I had some grapes. We switched some of them like usual. We were talking about the Vampire Diaries.

Personally, I'm on team Damon. Evelyn, on the other hand, is in love with Stefan.

"Hey," Erik interrupted us sliding in besides me.

"Hi," I said looking to Evelyn for help.

Evelyn just shrugged and smiled.

"Hey handsome, come to sweep me off my feet?" Evelyn joked.

I gave her my shut up look.

"Maybe, that depends. Let me check my schedule." Erik joked back.

"I'll wait," Evelyn said.

I rolled my eyes at the both of them.

"What were you guys talking about?" Erik asked leaning over towards me.

"The Vampire Diaries."

He laughed, "That show? Do you really believe in vampires?"

"Of course I do, and I have a unicorn in my backyard."

Evelyn almost spit her water all over the table.

"You're so stupid," she said.

Erik shook his head and laughed at us. He probably thinks we are so immature.

"Seriously, if you met a vampire what would you do?"

"I don't know, run away," I giggled.

Flashback

"What? Why would you run away?"

"Because, I vouldn't vant heem to suck my blood," I said in my Dracula voice.

Erik obviously didn't think I was funny. "Not all vampires suck people's blood you know, they have blood bags," he said seriously.

"Okay, what are you a vampire connoisseur?" Evelyn asked, laughing.

The bell rang. Lunch was over. I didn't even get to ask him what he was going to tell me tomorrow.

After Lunch I had Graphic design class. Rachael is in my class, but since she was sick, I was all alone. I have a bunch of affluent, snobby kids in class that I don't even talk to. My teacher, Ms. DellaValle, is awesome. She is like the best teacher I have ever had. She always thinks my design work is really good. Even though I usually think it sucks. Our assignment was to make a website using Dreamweaver. I started off making my page all black with red dripping letters. It was obviously a tribute to the Vampire Diaries, since I am addicted to that show. I didn't get a chance to finish it before the bell rang again. I had study hall right before last period. No one is in my study either so I usually just text my friends and hope they don't get in trouble.

My phone vibrated in my pocket. The caller ID said

"anonymous." I answered it even though we are not really supposed to.

"Hello." No one answered back. "Hello," I said again quietly. I just heard breathing.

"Whatever," I said annoyed and hung up.

The phone rang again with the anonymous number. I picked it up again. No one was there. I was getting ticked. I turned my phone off.

I didn't even study; I just doodled in my notebook. I kept drawing the same trees over and over again. The time passed slowly, and I couldn't wait to go to Drama class.

Erik was already in class when I got to the music room. He looked like he was kissing up to the teacher. I didn't know what they were talking about but the teacher apparently thought he was funny.

The rest of the class strolled in. We had to practice for the end of the year show, which was a musical version of Shakespeare's *A Midsummer Night's Dream.* I already tried out and got the role Hermia in it. I wondered if Erik would get a part even though he just joined. I didn't even know if he was a good singer or not.

The teacher said that she needed some guys to come forward for the part of Lysander. Erik raised his hand to sing. I couldn't wait to hear his voice; I bet he sings like an angel.

Flashback

She handed him a piece of paper with the lyrics to some song I have never heard. "Swift as a shadow, short as any dream…" He began to sing.

OH MY GOD! He sucked. It was awful. He was monotone and way off beat. Everyone in the class just stared at him. The teacher somewhat applauded. I just stood there with my hand over my mouth in disbelief. He still looked hot even though he sounded like an idiot.

"Okay, next?" The teacher said.

Aidan got up and sang next. He was really good, and would probably get the part. I hope he does because the only other choice was Arnold and he spits when he talks.

After school I went straight home. I had an essay about propaganda due for English class so I wanted to finish it before my date with Erik. I worked on it all afternoon.

Chapter 9: Sisters

I sat on my bed and played "Holiday" by Green Day on my guitar. My sister walked into my room to see what I was doing.

"What's up Iz? No, plans on a Friday night?"

"Uh, no Rachael is sick and Evelyn has a family birthday party, and they're like my only friends. Doesn't look like you have much to do either?"

"I was just coming in to see if you want to go out with me."

I was astonished. Jocelyn never invites me to do anything because she thinks I am still a kid. "Are you serious?"

"Yeah, my friend Cole is a bouncer at Liquid and there is a good band playing there tonight. They play all that weird Green Day stuff you like."

I jumped up and hugged her. "Thank you, thank you! Oh my God what am I going to wear?"

Jocelyn laughed, "I am going to get changed we have like 15 minutes to get ready. I am telling mom and dad we are going to the movies."

*

We arrived at the club and I was so nervous they weren't going to let me in because it was 18 and over. But I tried to look older with my skinny jeans and boots pulled over them. Cole was at the door and just let us right in. I felt like such a rebel. The club was packed and we could barely get through the crowd. Jocelyn was looking for her friends, Alexis and Gia.

The band sounded awesome. The song, "What I've Done," blared through the speakers.

Alexis ran up to us. "Hey we've been looking all over for you. This place is crazy. I can't believe you brought your little sister here."

I put my hands on my hips, "I'm not that much younger than you."

"I know," she said.

Flashback

"Let's dance," Gia squealed as she grabbed my sister's hand and pulled her onto the dance floor. Her long dark hair practically hit me in the face.

We got on the dance floor and I saw London right smack in the middle of it. I didn't even pay much attention to her because I didn't want it to ruin my night.

I had such a good time with my sister. Maybe now she would treat me like an adult.

Chapter 10: Love Letter

I was in my room brushing my hair. I kept looking in my mirror trying to compare myself to a sketch of my mother that I stuck to my mirror. I didn't see a resemblance, except for the hair. Nothing else reminded me of her. Her smile was beautiful, mine was not. Her eyes were wide and happy. Mine were dull. I absolutely did not see what James or my father were talking about. James said she even lit up the room when she walked in, and when she smiled everyone would instantly be happy. And he could never forget her laugh; he said it was contagious. I wish my mother could be here. If I were sad, she would be sitting on my bed, stroking my hair and telling me everything was okay. If she were here I probably wouldn't be betrothed to Nathan.

Flashback

"Katherine," My father called from outside my door.

"Yes father," I called getting up to open it.

My father was standing there with a letter in his hand. My father's a nice man even though he betrothed me to *that pig.* I don't think he knew what he was getting me into. For all I know he probably thought Nathan was a very nice boy with a lot of money. He only wanted the best for me, but I guess his plan backfired. He just didn't know it.

There's a letter for you," he said handing it to me.

"Thank you," I said taking it.

"Well, I have to get going, the cows aren't going to sell themselves," he said walking away chuckling to himself.

I shut the door and walked over to my bed. I stared at the envelope for a minute, my hands trembled. It felt like there was something inside.

The envelope had my name scrawled out in cursive:

$$\mathcal{K}atherine.$$

I opened the envelope, and inside laid a necklace as well as a letter. The necklace had a moon and a couple of diamonds around it. I instantly put it on and then read the letter.

My Dearest Katherine,

I can't get over the night we shared together at the mayor's ball two nights ago. I'd like to see you again. . I know I have just met you but I can't shake this feeling that we belong together. Since that night I can't stop thinking about you, can't stop dreaming about you. I have been falling in love with you more and more every day. I know it sounds insane, but it's true. And I have a feeling that you feel this way, too. If so, meet me by the lake today at noon. I look forward to seeing you.

Forever and always,

Erik

Flashback

I have been feeling exactly what he wrote. It's like he read my mind. And he wants to meet me at noon? I looked at Daniel's pocket watch and it was in 15 minutes! I quickly looked myself over in my mirror and ran out the door. I almost made it outside when James stopped me.

"Whoa, where are you going in such a hurry?" He asked.

What am I going to say to him?

"I'm going to the market. I heard from Lillian that they just got some new fabric to make dresses. I have to hurry if I want to get the good fabrics," I lied.

I hated lying to James; if I weren't going to see Erik I would feel guilty.

"Okay, well be sure to save some for me," he joked.

"Yeah, ha-ha," I fake-laughed.

I'm not sure he bought it, but he let me leave anyway.

I went to our red barn, and went to get my horse, Midnight.

There are two reasons why I named him that. One, he is black and beautiful. Two, I found him at midnight with my brothers once, when we were fooling around against my father's wishes.

I put a saddle on him, and hopped on. I wasn't going to walk to the lake; it's in the woods.

Nobody ever goes in those woods alone.

We rode halfway into the woods when the horse stopped.

"Come on Midnight, walk," I demanded.

The horse neighed in response and shook his head.

"Well then," I said getting off and tying him to a tree. "Stay here and I'll come back for you later."

I walked farther into the woods, and I heard something following me. I looked back and there was nothing. I kept on walking. I heard the footsteps advancing. I ran quickly, eager to get to the lake. If there was a chance that someone was following me, I could just jump in the lake. Or if I were lucky, Erik would be there.

I got to the lake, and no one was there. Did he lie to me? Or did he just not get there yet? I felt a little nervous. Then somebody quickly grabbed me. I screamed. I turned and saw it was Erik. I started to cry.

"Hey, it's okay, I was only kidding, I thought you would laugh," he said pulling me towards him.

I stopped my fake tears. I learned to do that over the years with my brothers, it works every time. "That's for scaring me half to death," I said slapping him on his arm light enough so it wouldn't hurt. I wasn't really mad. My brothers try to scare me all the time.

He laughed, "Fine, I'll accept my punishment."

"Where's my sorry?" I asked pointing to my lips.

He laughed again and kissed me. He pulled back.

"You're wearing the necklace," He said pointing to it.

"Yes," I said clutching it in my hand.

"That was my mother's; I thought it would be perfect for you."

"It is, it's beautiful."

"Well I'm glad you like it."

We lay in the grass for a while and talked. My head lay on his chest, and his hand stroked my hair. It felt so comfortable with him, so natural.

"Do you want to go for a swim?" He asked trying to pull me off the grass into the lake.

"I can't, I told my brother I was going to the market."

I wished I could. I just wanted to have fun with someone else besides my brothers.

We sat a little longer talking. I told him about my mother, and he told me about his. His parents died when he was three, and he's being raised by his aunt and uncle. His uncle was a merchant overseas so he was not home that much.

"I am so sorry to hear about your parents. I guess I'm lucky to have two brothers."

"You are, and they love you very much."

He was so gentle and kind when he talked. He made me feel comfortable and important.

We talked a while longer, and with each word he spoke I could feel myself falling in love. I could picture myself in his arms for eternity. Being married, living a life together and having children together. It made me angry to think I would have to marry Nathan.

"I have to go," I said, really not wanting to leave, ever.

"Okay, I'll take you home."

We went to get my horse, and I hopped up. He untied him for me, held the reins and walked next to me while I rode.

When we got close to my house we stopped. He went to leave, but then he jumped up on the stirrups instead. He kissed me. It was wonderful, and my body tingled all over.

"Goodbye, my sweet Katherine," he whispered in my ear.

"Goodbye, Erik."

He jumped back down and started to walk away.

"Wait," I called.

"Yes," He asked.

"Tomorrow, meet me in the meadow at noon."

"Okay," he said smiling so happily that I couldn't help but smile back.

He started to walk away once more but I yelled to him again.

"I love you!" I can't believe I blurted that out. I've only known him for like a day. This was all happening so fast.

"I love you too," He called without looking back.

Chapter 11: Truth and Lies

Erik showed up at my house at 2:00pm. I didn't know how he knew my address, but I didn't care. He beeped the horn. I rushed to finish putting my makeup on and I ran down the stairs. I hoped my makeup didn't look like crap. I ripped the door open with such enthusiasm I probably looked like a dork. When I got outside the first thing I saw was his car. It's a sliver V12 Vantage Aston Martin. I have never been in such an expensive car in my life. I felt like I was little orphan Annie. I wanted to tell him about the dream I had the night before, but I knew I couldn't.

"Hi," he said as he rolled down the window. Before I could say anything he was out of the car and opening my door for me. I got in the car and just said, "Hey," like an idiot.

"Ready to go, babe?" He asked.

"Yeah," I replied with a big stupid grin on my face.

As soon as I drove out of the driveway I freaked.

"Why the hell are you driving so fast?" I yelled.

"Sorry." He mumbled as he slowed down. "It's nothing like driving a horse and carriage."

I laughed.

Even after we slowed down we were still going really fast. We barely talked in the car. I didn't know if I was nervous or happy, so I didn't want to start a conversation.

We got to the beach in less than two minutes.

As soon as we got out of the car he said very seriously, "I need to talk to you."

"About what?" I said nervously as we walked down the cement stairs onto the beach.

"Everything!" Erik said, kicking the shells in the sand.

My mind raced. What the hell was everything I wondered? He knew I was Katherine, right? Why else would he feel this connection with me? I was so anxious. We walked across the hot sand, took off our flip-flops and walked into the water. We started strolling down the beach hand in hand. Our hands just kind of slipped into one another's. It felt so natural.

"I'm Katherine." I blurted out.

He looked at me confused. "Yeah, I knew it was you, Katherine, I need to tell you everything."

Oh my God. How many times was he going to say

that? "So, spill," I said getting impatient.

"Okay let me sum it up this way..." he looked nervous for once. "Well, um, I am a vampire."

"What the hell, Erik." I screamed, "Is this some kind of sick joke?"

A freakin vampire? They are not real. He's kidding, right? Vampires only exist in books like the *Vampire Diaries,* or the *Mortal Instruments* series. Not in real life. Or do they?

A tingling feeling went over my whole body. I was numb for a minute. How is that summing it up? I had loved a vampire for all those years. Why didn't he tell me, why did he hide it? No way is this happening to me!

"I'm afraid it's not a joke. But just hear me out. I thought my life was over when I turned, but then I met you."

He took a long pause.

"And then, then you were killed." His voice got quieter. "I swore to kill whoever did it and for all these years I have been looking for them. I never found out who it was but I know they are still alive today. I was a couple of miles away from here looking and I felt you. I realized you were somehow alive. I came rushing here to find you. I watched you from afar not knowing it was you. As I got closer, the feeling got stronger. I wasn't a hundred percent sure it was you until I talked to you at school."

Flashback

I was speechless. I stared at him blankly. How dare he hide these things from me and then just come out and say it like it was no big deal? Well, it is to me.

"Say something," he pleaded.

"I..." I stuttered. He looked heartbroken so I decided not to scream at him. "Why didn't you tell me?" I said trying not to make my voice waver, but of course it didn't work.

"I didn't want to hurt you," he said carefully.

Forget it. I was trying to subside my anger, but it wasn't working. "What the hell! You did hurt me. You hurt me by lying to me." I screamed waving my hands up in the air.

"You don't understand," he said.

"What don't I understand that you're a lying, vampire, jerk?"

I hated how he sounded so calm when the situation so obviously wasn't.

"I didn't want to tell you, and have you look at me everyday like I was a monster." His voice quivered a bit. Finally, he was showing some emotion, I mean really is he a rock? I felt guilty for yelling at him and my heart raced. I was confused and angry and I just wanted to leave.

He wrapped his arm around me and with his other hand he held mine. His touch made my whole body calm. I turned and kissed him. He kissed me back. I felt the same way I did the first time I kissed him. Like a spaz. The kiss was amazing. The brush of his lips against mine made my heart pound and I didn't want it to end. Unfortunately it had to, and ironically I'm the one who pushed away.

"I love you." He whispered in my ear. And again like the spaz I am, I said, "I need to go home." No I love you too or kissing him again. I needed to go home. Any other girl would have loved to stay and walk on the beach with a gorgeous guy. I just couldn't handle it. I couldn't just pick up where we left off. I had died. I had a new life that he hasn't been a part of. I still felt betrayed. I couldn't talk about it anymore.

"Okay, I'll take you home," he said kindly.

That's it! He was just going to take me home? No questions asked. Was he unfazed? How come I can never read his emotions? Was he hurt?

We walked back to the stairs that lead up to the parking lot. I brushed the sand off my feet with my hands and put my flip-flops back on. I hadn't even taken my clothes off to show off my new teal bikini. Rachael was going to be so mad at me. As we were getting in the car I could see a group of girls staring at us and laughing. I am sure they were wondering why a hottie like Erik was with a loser like me.

Flashback

Chapter 12: Bad News

We pulled up to my house; the car ride had been silent. I got out of the car and said, "Thanks for the ride." In my head I said, "I love you, too." His eyes opened wide as if he knew what I said.

"I know Katherine, I mean Iz. Can I pick you up for school Monday?"

"Sure." Is all I said back as I shut the door and walked toward my house.

This day had already been crazy, what I didn't know was that it was about to get worse. I opened the front door and all hell broke loose. My mother and sister were sitting, sobbing on the couch.

I didn't know why they were crying, but I knew something horrible had happened.

"Oh my God!" Mom sobbed, rushing over to me, "thank God you're home."

"Mom, calm down, it's okay, what happened?"

"Your father…" she could barely get the words out. "He's dead."

The words hit me like a punch in the stomach. I dropped to my knees and cradled my head with my hands. He was dead. He couldn't be. He is supposed to be here for me. To tell me boys are no good. Help heal my broken heart. Watch me graduate from college. Walk me down the aisle. The life we were supposed to share together flashed through my head. "How did it happen?" I shrieked, blinking back the tears. I would not cry. It was hard trying not to start bawling my eyes out. But I managed. I would save that for when I was alone.

"A fire at his work. They don't know how it started, but there were no survivors in his department," Jocelyn said.

"I'll be right back," I said as I got up and went right back out the door. I didn't know where I was going but I didn't care. I just needed to be alone. I wondered why they didn't call me, but then I saw that my phone was off. I turned it on and saw fifteen missed calls, and a text message from my Dad that read:

I love you -Tell your mother and sister too

It was from 2:15 P.M. today. It must have been right before he died. Maybe he knew what was coming. The thought of that made me cry and I began to run.

I kept running until I got to the place my Dad and I would go when I was little. I didn't know the name of it, but I knew exactly where it was. It was our secret place. It was a wooded area about a half a mile from our house. There used to be a white bench just in the middle of all the big trees, but it wasn't there anymore. I sat on the leaves and sobbed for what seemed like hours. It had actually only been 30 minutes when somebody found me.

I looked up and saw a guy my age. He was wearing jeans and a red Abercrombie shirt. He had black wavy hair and chocolate brown eyes. His eyes looked concerned.

"Are you okay?" He asked.

"Yes." I said wiping the tears from my eyes.

"I'm Chris." He said, his eyes looking me over with apprehension. His voice had an unusual familiarity to me, but I didn't recognize him.

"I'm Isabelle." I said trying to perk up and act like I didn't just find out my father died.

"Pretty." He said with a smile on his face. "Are you sure you're all right?" He asked again. "Don't be afraid to tell me."

This guy seemed honest and trustworthy. Like him and I were long lost friends. I just began to tell him everything

Flashback

that had happened that day. Somewhere in the middle of it I started crying again. He pulled me close and started hugging me and telling me it was okay. I don't know why I felt so comforted by a stranger. I usually do not let my guard down. Maybe I just needed someone to cry to, anyone.

"I am sorry to burden you with this. I don't even know you," I said wiping my eyes.

"It's okay, I don't know what it is like to lose a parent, but my parents just got divorced so I moved here from New York. I have been feeling really alone lately, too. I go to Carlsbad High School and I don't know many people."

"I go there too, I don't think I have ever seen you but you do look indistinctly familiar."

"Really?" He said raising his eyebrows with a smirk on his face. "So do you, but not just from the hallways in school, from a distant memory I suppose?" He laughed.

"Exactly! But maybe I'm just imagining things?"

"Maybe?"

He made me feel so much better; I wanted to hang with him again. We swapped phone numbers and I headed home.

Chapter 13: More Lies

When I got home I locked myself in my room and didn't respond to anyone for days. All of my friends called to check on me (and when I say all I mean Rachael and Evelyn). I didn't want to talk to anyone. I just laid in my bed and cried for hours on end. I couldn't even think about eating.

My mom left me alone, but my sister kept banging on my door. Why couldn't she just go to college and stop bothering me? "Go away Jocelyn!" I yelled every time. I was so depressed about my dad I couldn't talk to anyone about him, not even my sister. Once again she knocked annoyingly on the door.

"Go away Jocelyn, leave me alone!" She didn't listen this time. She opened the door and I threw a pillow at her. Seriously, what if I had been changing or something? She thinks she can just come in my room anytime she wants, like she's the Queen of England. Hell no! It is something called privacy! But my pillow plan didn't work. She caught the pillow in one slick movement. "Really? A Pillow?" Said a voice. It wasn't my sister after all. It was Erik. Not that I was annoyed he was there, I was ecstatic really, but he had barged right in.

"Yeah, now what do you want?" I said. It came out harsher then I intended it to be, but he is a big boy and he can handle it.

"Wow, cruel," he said sarcastically. "I just wanted to see if my girlfriend is okay."

Girlfriend! Was this a joke?! Cause if it was, vampire or not, I'd give him hell.

"Really?" I asked, trying not to sound too excited. It didn't work.

He just smiled and said, "Seriously."

"Well, thanks for coming, but I am fine."

He lay next to me on my bed and brushed my hair away from my eyes. "Reeeallly?" He said. He was obviously not buying it when I said I was okay. "No." I sighed.

"Well, you look like crap."

"Thanks," I rolled my eyes. "That helps a lot," I said defensively.

"I know," he said looking smug. I was glad he came. He made me feel better.

"I'm glad I came too," he said. What! That's the second time he did that to me. Maybe he can read my mind. I'm so glad he told me that. Oh my God. I hope he didn't read all my embarrassing thoughts. That's just great.

"Yes, all vampires can read thoughts and communicate telepathically."

I just stared at him too angry to talk. I didn't even want to think because I didn't want him to know all the mean things I was thinking about him. He was just making me so mad.

"If you're really that mad I can teach you how to shield your thoughts."

I jumped. He said it in my mind and that's what scared me.

"That was telepathy or as I like to call it mindspeak," he laughed.

"Oh," I said embarrassed. "So teach me."

"I can teach you how to shield your thoughts from vampires, but humans cannot mind-speak,"

"Why not?" I thought trying to mindspeak, knowing it wasn't going to work.

Laughing he said, "Ummm, did you just speak telepathically to me, or was that just my imagination? How did you do that, you're not supposed to be able to!" He said

70   **Flashback**

quizzically. He was happy and silly today. He was like Rachael, but less annoying.

"Yes, I am happy and thanks for the comparison," he said. "Now if you don't want me to read your mind, I suggest you let me teach you."

"I'm ready, but to answer your question, I really don't know." Maybe he could teach me how to block the sadness of my dad's passing out of my mind. He was actually making me forget how upset I was.

"Picture a wall in your mind."

"How is that going to work?" I said doubtingly.

"Just picture the freakin wall," he said sighing.

So, I did. I pictured a bright blue wall with yellow writing on it that says, "Do not enter Erik!" It was so thick and tall that it would take a bulldozer to break through it.

Surprisingly it worked. In a matter of minutes he couldn't read my mind. I was so excited. Maybe everything I thought about vampires was true.

"So, Summerland is a real place?" I asked, hoping my dream of Alyson Noel's *Immortal Series* being real was true. I am a believer, what can I say!

"No," he laughed.

"Thanks for crushing my dream," I exaggerated with my hand over my forehead like I was in an old drama film. He just laughed.

"So, there's no Volturi, or Originals?" I asked, hoping my beliefs weren't going to be destroyed.

"Iz, there Is no Volturi like in the *Twilight Saga*, no originals from the *Vampire Diaries,* and no Summerland from *Evermore.* Just vampires, werewolves, and witches."

"So, you have read the books," I said raising my eyebrows.

"Yes," he said pulling me towards him. "But they aren't as great as ours will be," he said whispering in my ear, which made me blush. He kissed me, but I pulled back and totally ruined the moment. Of course like an idiot, I made the situation even less romantic and asked, "Do you have any idea who my killer is?"

His head dropped, "No."

I don't know why he got so upset when we talked about this. I was right in front of him, still alive. Maybe it was the thought of losing me again. My killer was still alive, it could most likely happen again.

"Sorry, for asking," I said dropping my head down, too.

"It's okay," he said lifting my chin up.

"No, it's not," I replied, tears welling up in my eyes, and not even for that reason.

"Why are you crying?"

I turned my head away, not wanting to tell him why. I wasn't so sure I was right about my idea.

"Isabelle," he said seriously, "look at me and tell me what is making you so upset, now I can't read your mind, you're getting good at this."

I paced back and forth in front of my bed. Reluctantly, I locked his eyes with mine and told him. How did we get on this subject? One minute I was fantasizing about my favorite books being real and the next I was telling him about what I thought really happened to my father.

"I think my father was purposely killed."

"What!" He said obviously taken aback.

"I said..."

"I know what you said," he said cutting me off. "I just want to know why you think that."

"He sent me a text right before he died like he knew what was coming."

"Let me see the text," he said.

I grabbed my phone and threw it to him. He caught it in one graceful movement.

"Sooooo?" I asked dragging out the word. I was curious what he thought about the text and what he thought might have happened to my father.

"I think you're right!"

Terrific! I was proud of myself for being right, but I also didn't want to be right. I didn't want it to be my killer. What if he stays and keeps killing until he gets me. I was dreading what could happen next.

"It's him, I feel it!" Erik continued, "He's here."

"Yeah, no crap," I said sarcastically.

"Isabelle, this is serious," he said. "We don't know who he is, he could be anyone. We need to be careful and not trust anyone."

"What about my friends?"

"You can't tell them Iz."

"But..." my words choked up.

"Isabelle, no buts or else..."

"Or what? You'll kill me? Already been through that before. Got anything new?" I said laughing half-heartedly.

Ignoring that he continued, "Or else I will lock you in your room until you've gotten some sense knocked into you."

"You can't tell me I have to stay in my room. You're not my father! Because I don't even have a father anymore – he's dead! You're just my sorry-ass boyfriend who thinks he can come in here and tell me what to do like a freakin father. You don't control me!"

"Iz..."

Flashback

"Don't call me that!" I screamed. "You know what? Just leave!"

"Iz…. Calm down, please…"

"I said LEAVE!"

And he did. He left. He turned around and left. I watched him run down the stairs and slam the door on his way out. I couldn't believe he actually left. I slammed my bedroom door so hard my painting of Picasso's *The Dream* fell onto the floor. I looked at it, didn't pick it up, and just flung my body onto my bed. I starting crying, crying about my dad and the fact that I just spazzed on Erik for no real reason. Part of me wanted him to stay, but the other part didn't. After hours of feeling sorry for myself I decided to text Chris:

Hi

A minute later he replied:

Hey ☺

Whatsupp? I text back.

Just at boring school, it's a Tuesday remember?

Oh yeah (I couldn't keep track of the days anymore)

So, when will you be back in school? I would like to pick you up one day.

Thursday, if I am up to it. Tomorrow's my dad's funeral. I really can't believe I have to face this. It doesn't feel real.

I responded.

> *I know Iz. You'll get through this. So it's a date then? Can I drive you home too?*

> *Definitely. Thank you!*

I texted back in like a second.

Great! GTG Mr. Barnes caught me- text you later. Oh and BTW I got the part of Demetrius!

I couldn't help by smile. I faded off to sleep.

Chapter 14: Intuition

I saw thick black smoke and bright flames filling a hallway. I heard people screaming. There was a voice in the distance, it sounded like my father, but it couldn't be. He's dead.

I was in a familiar office building. I walked closer to the voice, the fire wasn't hurting me, and I could breathe just fine. I saw my dad's secretary, Janet; she tried to open the fire exit.

"Janet," I called after her.

She didn't even acknowledge that I called her. She cried because she couldn't get the door open. It was jammed shut. I walked over to her and put my arm out to help but my hand went right through her. Was she a ghost?

I walked a little further where I saw a bunch of my dad's business associates. They were all screaming frantically.

Flashback

One of them was trying to break the window with a computer chair. I finally realized I was at my dad's office. I started running, trying to find my father. Maybe I could save him.

As I got closer to my father's office I could see him through the window. His normally perfect slicked back blonde hair was tousled. His big blue eyes were tearing up. He threw his cell phone on the desk and started screaming. "Damn it, he will not win! I will not let him hurt her."

I waved my hands in front of him screaming, "Dad I am here," trying to get his attention. But he couldn't hear or see me. There was nothing I could do. I watched him run out of his office, screaming to get everyone's attention. I saw his cell phone on his desk, so I picked it up and read it. The message read:

If I die, contact Evelyn. She'll know what to do.

Why would he ask someone to contact Evelyn?

Chapter 15: Funeral

When I finally woke up I realized it was the day of my father's funeral and the dream I just had may give me some insight into my father's death. I wondered why he would have wanted someone to contact Evelyn? I couldn't worry about that now.

My Dad was burned so badly in the fire we couldn't have a proper wake for him. It took all my strength to get out of bed and get ready for my Dad's service. I didn't want my friends to come and I especially did not want Erik to see me like this again.

I threw on my old, short, black halter-top silk dress. The same one I have worn to many family occasions. My black heals were so worn down that my left leg was higher than the right. I decided to borrow a pair of flats from my sister.

Flashback

I went into Jocelyn's room. She had on a similar dress. Too bad we looked nothing alike in it. My sister looked really pretty. Her silky blonde hair was down in waves. And her body looked way more voluptuous than mine in her tight black dress. I looked liked I was wearing something of my mother's, that didn't fit.

"Do you want me to do your hair, sis?" She asked. This was the first time she had talked to me in days.

I handed her a beautiful clip that was my grandmother's and told her to put my hair back in it, just the way my dad liked it.

My mom walked in. "How do I look my girls?"

She had a white blouse and a black skirt on. Her ageless face looked like it had aged twenty years. I knew it would go back to normal eventually.

When we got to the church it seemed like forever before the priest started and it felt like eternity before it ended. This was the church my parents got married in and my sister and I were baptized in. It has always been a happy place for our family and today its bright stain glassed windows seemed dark and dull to me. The gold that lined the walls on the light blue altar didn't seem to shine as brightly anymore. I didn't know how I could return to the church for anything else.

Many people spoke at the service. My great aunt Rita went on and on about how she taught him how to sail and make banana bread. It made me happy to hear such wonderful things about my father's childhood. My mom cried the entire time and Jocelyn and I sat on each side of her, holding her hands. My mother had to be held up in our arms to walk out of the church.

It only took a couple of minutes to get to the cemetery. The hole was dug for his urn and his tombstone was already there. We were all in a circle around the plot. Rachael, Evelyn and Erik were directly across from me, but I barely lifted my head to look at them. When the priest finished they lowered the urn into the ground and everyone paid their respects and walked to their cars. We were the last to do it. My mom started bawling her eyes out again the second we started, and Jocelyn did too. I didn't. I wanted to be strong. I needed to be the sane one, the one who keeps this family together while we're going through this. I'd save it for when I'm alone.

When it was time to go I wouldn't leave. I just stared at the flowers and tombstone.

"Iz, you coming?" Jocelyn asked.

"No," I said without looking up.

"But, how will you get home?"

"I'll walk," I said flatly.

"You sure? It's not that close."

"I'll be fine."

"Okay, bye Iz." She left reluctantly.

When she left I stood there in front of the grave sobbing into my hands. I had never cried so much in my life (at least this life.) Finally, I couldn't take standing anymore. I sat down leaning against my father's stone, until the world went black around me.

*

It was almost noon and my dad hadn't left the house yet. I was getting nervous that he would catch Erik coming over to see me. My brothers were already in town selling our vegetables. Dad was still home because one of the horses looked sick. He had been trying to nurse her back to health all morning. He realized he couldn't help her and needed to go into town to bring the vet to our home.

He took Midnight and rode off down the road. Two

minutes later I looked in the back and saw Erik already in the meadow by a big oak tree.

I ran out of the house as fast as I could straight into his arms. He stroked his hand through my hair and said. "You're hair is so soft and beautiful, just like the rest of you. Do you know that?"

"Oh, Erik, how I've missed you."

"You too my darling."

We sat down on the grass in front of the big oak tree. It was a warm spring day, the sun gleamed and a soft breeze swayed the dry grass. We watched cute bunnies and chipmunks come up and eat the grass. I brought some stale bread to throw to the birds. Erik took it from my hand and tossed it really far. A flock of sparrows came down and fought over it.

It was so blissful and calm. I wanted to spend the rest of my life doing this. If I married Nathan, my life would be nothing like this. I would have to shoot birds, not feed them. I dreaded the thought and shivered.

"What's wrong?" Erik asked.

"Nothing," I lied. I didn't want to tell him that I was thinking about Nathan right then.

"You can tell me anything you know," he said caressing my hair. "I won't judge you, believe me, I know what you feel like," He muttered quietly to himself.

I knew I could, I confided in him more than anyone.

"It's not that important."

"Tell me please," He pleaded.

"Fine," I sighed, "I was thinking about Nathan. I don't want to marry him Erik, I just can't! You saw the way he treated me that night. Save me from him again just like you did then," I cried.

"I will, I'll try to figure it out soon."

"Thank you," I said smiling and relieved.

He kissed me. It was staggering. His lips were warm and soft. He made me feel special and wanted. I loved being with him. I loved him. He would make me much happier than Nathan. I wished it were him I was betrothed to.

James came into the meadow and saw me and Erik together. Now I was going to have to explain how much I care about him. James is not going to believe me. He would still want me to obey my father's wishes. He just looked at us and walked away.

Chapter 16: Blackouts

I woke up in the cemetery and it was dark. I picked up my phone. It was 9:00 P.M.; I had been there for 5 even hours. I had to get home. I didn't want to walk all the way home in the dark so I ran to catch the last bus. When I got there the bus was about to leave, but the driver saw my distress and stopped to let me in. I put my money in the slot and took a seat. I saw myself in the big mirror above his head, and I looked like a wreck. My hair was all messed up, my make-up was smeared on the side of my face and my dress was all muddy. I couldn't wait to get home.

When I walked in the house my mom was sleeping on my Dad's favorite recliner. Her feet hung over the footrest that was so worn out from dad's work boots always rubbing against it. Her head nuzzled in the pillow that hung over the back of the chair as if she was smelling it when she fell asleep.

Flashback

My sister was making food in the kitchen. She heard me come in and walked into the living room.

"What the hell happened to you?" Her eyes were opened so wide.

"I fell asleep in the cemetery."

She laughed and said, "Only you."

Yeah, if she only knew.

"Oh and that guy Erik called, said you weren't answering his texts and ignoring his calls."

"Yeah." I said.

"What happened?" She eyed me suspiciously.

"Nothing, I'm going to bed, night."

"And he..." I was already up the stairs before she could finish.

When I got to my room Erik was sitting on my bed, strumming my guitar. "I didn't know you play the guitar," he said without looking up.

"You, don't know a lot about me. How'd you get in here anyway?" I said, my voice cold.

"Your sister, we spoke on the phone and she let me come over."

I was shocked. "What did you say to her?"

"I wanted to talk to you, and..."

"But I don't want to talk to you," I cut him off.

Flashback

"Iz…" he said finally looking up. "You look like a mess! What the hell happened to you? Are you okay?" He asked, his face softening. "I was worried about you."

"I'm fine Erik, there's nothing to worry about. You didn't have to come here."

"Why, do you not want me here?" He said wiping my mascara off the side of my face.

"Not right now Erik. Why don't you just go." I said removing his hand from my cheek.

"Fine Iz, if that's what you really want."

"I do Erik; I just want to go to bed." I hugged him quickly.

He kissed my forehead and said, "Goodnight." He didn't seem too happy he had to go.

I am sure he thinks I am bipolar but I just wanted to be alone. I had other things on my mind than having to deal with my old vampire boyfriend. I took a nice long shower. Got in my comfy pink silk jammies, and drifted off into a dreamless sleep.

*

The next morning I woke up to a text from Chris, it said:

Be there in 20

K   I wrote back.

I had totally forgotten that he was coming.

I threw on a pair of ripped jeans that were lying on my floor and slipped my turquoise Hollister shirt over my bed-head. I hurried to brush my hair and slap on some makeup. As soon as I was done, I heard a car horn. I quickly grabbed my bag and ran downstairs and out the door. My mom and sister were still sleeping.

He was in a shiny, black Mercedes convertible, my dream car.

"Hey," he said.

"Hi," I said smiling.

I must have been standing there like a dork because he said, "Don't just stand there." He laughed. "Get in the car."

So, I got in the car and realized he was listening to one of my favorite songs, "I Just Wanna Run" by the Downtown Fiction. "I love this song," I said.

"Me too!" He said with excitement. I smiled at him and he smiled back.

"So are you feeling better about, you know…" he

asked, his voice trailing off.

Is he talking about Erik? How the heck does he know? "Bout what?' I asked stupidly.

"Uh, your dad," he said.

"Oh that?" I muttered, trying not to tear up.

"I'm sorry, I didn't mean to get you upset," he said.

"No, it's okay," I said as we pulled into the school parking lot.

Wow, I didn't realize he drove faster than Erik.

"Just know I am here for you," he said parking the car.

He got out of the car and walked around to the other side of the car and opened the door for me.

"I thought chivalry died when I did," I giggled to myself. "Thanks, Chris."

"Welcome. Let's go," he said walking towards the building.

I followed him and saw Erik watching us. I was yearning to go to him, but I felt stupid to just walk up to him. So, I didn't.

Rachael and Evelyn were next to my locker obviously waiting to attack me with a bunch of questions. I figured I might as well get it over with.

"Are you okay?" Evelyn asked pulling me into a tight hug, not even noticing Chris was with me.

Flashback

"Yeah, but you're kind of choking me."

"Sorry," Evelyn pulled away laughing.

"How did he die?" Rachael asked quietly. "I'm sorry we didn't get to talk at the funeral."

"In a fire."

"Oh."

Wow, this was the quietest that Rachael had ever been, but I knew that wasn't going to last long. I didn't really want to get into my father's death at school. So I just asked them if we could talk about something else for now.

"So, what happened with you and Erik?" Rachael finally asked.

I was dreading the question. "Nothing," I answered.

"Really," Rachael raised her eyebrows. "Cause the day after your date he told me it went great. And he sits at our table now."

Evelyn chimed in, "He's sitting there today."

"What!"

"Yeah," Evelyn said.

I was ready to give them hell. Then the bell rang.

"Well we gotta go, see you second period," Evelyn said.

"Uh, Bye."

"What was that all about," Chris said from behind me.

I jumped; I totally forgot he was there.

"Just my friends being their usual crazy selves."

"So, you and Erik?" he asked. "I'm not really a big fan of him."

"No, not me and Erik, it lasted like a day."

"From my sources, more like a few weeks."

"Whatever, let's just get to class."

"Okay, I have first, second and last period with you," he said.

Math went by fast, but English was a living hell. Erik sat next to me, trying to talk to me. Chris sat behind me trying to listen to Erik. I just wanted to pay attention in class. We were talking about one of my favorite authors, F. Scott Fitzgerald. So, I was more interested in the teacher than two guys acting like idiots. Rachael and Evelyn were passing notes to each other. I think they were about me. I just wanted second period to be over.

I went to my next two classes before lunch. I don't have any of my friends in my Social Studies or Art class so I got a break from all the craziness. Art was enjoyable besides the fact I cannot draw, I can only sing.

Lunch was the worst! Chris waited for me at my locker then walked me to the café. When we got to the table Erik, Rachael and Evelyn were there talking.

"Hi," I said putting my lunch on the table.

"Hi," Erik said without looking up.

"Oh, by the way, who's this?" Evelyn asked brightly.

Before Chris or I could answer, Erik did. "Chris," he spat.

"Erik," I said sharply.

"Her new boyfriend," he continued.

I was upset with Erik but I would never choose anyone over him. We were going to make up eventually, right?

"Erik, please," I said with hurt in my voice.

"No, it's okay, go have fun with Chris."

"You know what? Just forget it. I'm leaving, so bye."

I picked my stuff up and turned around and walked away. I left Chris at the table yelling and swearing at Erik. I am not even sure what he was saying.

I ran out of the building and into the school parking lot. It would be a really good to have a car right now! Too much is happening in my life at once, my head pounded again. As if I wasn't devastated enough when my father died, I found out what Erik is and now he's mad at me. What else could go wrong? Oh, I forgot my killer is still alive! I wish everything could just go back to normal. Maybe even go back to my old life. It was easier then. Crap, why did I think that? Blackness filled the world around me like the day in the cemetery,

bringing me back. Back to my old life.

Flashback

Chapter 17: The Meadow

I was in the meadow with James, watching the clouds go by. Daniel of course was still reading in the study. We were lying in the grass with beautiful yellow flowers surrounding us. We gazed up at the sky and talked about our mother. I loved these times I had with James because he always talked about her.

"You remind me so much of mother. You have the same sweet voice as hers and the same mannerisms. And of course you are stubborn like her. Father always tried to tell her what to cook for dinner or how to take care of the hens and sheep, but she never listened. She went about things in her own way, just like you Katherine. I love being around you so much, because you make me remember her more."

Flashback

"I am glad you think that I am just like her," I said. "There is no one I'd rather be like more."

"Even your smile lights up the whole room like hers did."

"I wish she was here to meet Erik, she would like him. By the way Erik is coming at noon today before father gets back from town." I said to James.

"Really? You must have really hit it off at the ball," James laughed.

"All we did was dance."

"And kiss." I blushed at that.

James laughed, "You must really like him."

"Yes, I would marry him tomorrow if I could," I smiled.

"Over all the boys in town who like you, you pick him? Why?"

"You'll just laugh at me," I giggled.

"I promise I won't."

"Fine, do you believe in love at first sight?"

James started laughing hysterically and held his stomach.

"Well then," I said.

"I'm sorry, please go on."

"I'm done."

"Katherine, don't be that way."

"Katherine!" Daniel called out the back door, "Somebody is here for you."

"Do I look okay?" I asked James as I brushed little pieces of grass off my purple dress. He nodded.

"Thanks," I said touching my braided hair and running into the house.

"You're welcome, have fun," he called back.

I walked into the back door of the farmhouse. Erik was standing in the kitchen with Daniel. He looked just as handsome as the day I met him. He was leaning against the table that Dad and the boys had just built.

"Well don't just stand there, say hello to our guest." Daniel said.

"Hello, Erik." I curtsied.

"Good afternoon, Katherine," Erik replied.

"I'll go into the other room and let you catch up," Daniel said leaving us alone.

"I thought he'd never leave." Erik said pulling me closer to him.

"When are we going to tell my father and Daniel?"

Erik and I have been meeting secretly since I met him at the ball. My father would never approve because I am to marry Nathan. My father may disown me, but I am willing to take that chance for Erik. And Daniel may never speak to me again if I go against my father's wishes.

"Soon," he said whispering in my ear.

"Good, because I do not like lying to my family."

"I know, they don't like lying to you either."

"What are they lying to me about," I said pulling away from him.

"Nothing."

"Erik, tell me now."

"You wouldn't understand."

"What wouldn't I understand," I yelled.

"You wouldn't see me the same way," he muttered.

"Erik," I sighed defeated. "Tell me."

"No."

"Please," I pleaded.

I heard my father's voice outside.

Erik hugged me. "I can't now; we need to talk about it at another time. I need to go before your father sees me." He snuck out the back door.

My mind raced with a thousand questions that I'm not sure were ever even answered.

Chapter 18: What happened?

I woke up in a place I didn't recognize. The walls around me were blue and there were a lot of paintings hanging on them. I was on a brown couch with a yellow blanket draped over me. I saw an identical couch across from mine and there was a coffee table in the middle of the room. There was a nice flat screen TV on the wall.

"Where am I?" I asked myself expecting no one to answer.

"My house," said a man. Was it Erik? Did he bring me here to apologize?

"Erik?"

"No, Iz, it's Chris."

"Oh."

"Sorry to disappoint you," he said sarcastically.

"You didn't, what happened?"

"You ran out of the school and I went after you. I was going to ask you if you wanted me to bring you home. Before I could say anything you passed out in my arms. I put you in my car and brought you here so I could make sure you're alright."

"Oh," I said just thinking about what had happened in my dream. I mean it wasn't really a dream; it was a vision of my past life. I think it is ironic that we just had a fight at school and in my vision we had a similar argument. I couldn't stay mad at him for long in either situation.

"So do you know why you passed out?"

Should I tell him? Would he believe me? He will think I'm a lunatic. "No," I lied.

"Okay," he said obviously not buying it. "Anyway, I talked to Erik."

Yeah, more like yelled.

"And..." I pushed him to go on.

"He said he is sorry."

Was that it? Was that all he said, seriously? And why didn't he come to see if I was okay or tell me he was sorry in person?

"Okay, that's good. Oh no, what time is it?"

"Its 5:30 P.M., you've been asleep for 5 hours."

Wow, I thought I had only been out for like 30

minutes.

"Seriously?"

"Seriously," he said in a girlish voice, mocking me.

"Well, I really need to go."

"K, do you want me to drive you home?"

"Did I really forget that I don't have a car," I giggled.

"Do you need one?"

"Duh."

"I'll give you the Mercedes."

"What! To keep? No, no, no, you can't do that, that's your car."

"Seriously, it is fine, I was going to sell it anyway, it's a 2008. And besides, I have a Ferrari."

Oh my God, was this kid loaded or what? I didn't think it would be appropriate to ask him how he got all of these fancy cars. "You have a Ferrari? Why the hell do you drive a Mercedes?"

He just laughed.

"So, do you want the car or not?" He asked.

"Really, I don't know, are you sure?"

"Positive!"

"Then, YES!" I grinned widely.

"Good answer," he said throwing me the keys.

Thanks," I said. "For everything."

"Anytime."

"Bye," I said heading for the door.

"See ya later."

I walked out the door, heading for the car. I couldn't believe it was mine. "I freakin love him," I said out loud as I got in the car.

I pulled up to my house and my mom was sitting on the front porch waiting for me. My mom totally freaked out. Ever since my father passed she's been extra protective.

"Where were you?"

"At my friend's house."

"What friend? I've been trying to get a hold of you for hours. The school called and said you didn't go to any of your classes after lunch. Why didn't you call me Isabelle?"

"I didn't feel well so I went to Chris' house to rest. I just didn't feel like coming home."

"Who in the world is Chris?" She sounded annoyed.

"Just a friend of mine."

"Then who are you seeing?"

"Why do you think I am seeing someone, Mom?"

"Because I know you, and you have been acting different lately."

"Uh, I've been talking to Erik, but I am not sure what's going on anymore."

"Do you want to talk about it, honey?"

"No, not right now."

"Okay. Wait a second, whose car are you driving?"

"Mine."

"What! You bought a car! With what money?"

"No money, Chris gave it to me. He was going to sell it, but he knew I needed a car. So, he just gave it to me." I couldn't believe it myself. I have a car. I drive a Mercedes.

"I hope you thanked him, but I really don't think you should be accepting such an extravagant gift from a stranger. And who is going to pay for your insurance and everything else, miss?"

"Yes, I did. Can we not talk about this right now? Where's Jocelyn?" I asked finally realizing she wasn't here.

"Out with her friends, so it's just you and me for dinner. I really want to talk about this whole car thing Isabelle. I'm not sure I am okay with this yet." She said standing up and following me into the house.

My mom made chicken cutlets and had already set the kitchen table for the two of us. I really just wanted to go eat in my room but I knew my mom wanted the company. Dinner was two hours of my mother asking questions about school, my friends, Chris and Erik. I don't think she wanted to talk about my dad. I had a sixth sense that he was always on her mind. After dinner I headed to my room. I grabbed my guitar and started playing "Jar of Hearts" by Christina Perri. It felt like a good song for the moment. When I was done playing I got in the shower and then went to bed. I fell asleep instantly; I didn't realize how tired I was.

"Erik, Erik, Erik," I whimpered in my sleep.

I then felt someone stroking my hair. I opened my eyes and saw it was him.

"Erik," I cried.

"Shhh." He put his finger over my lips and lay on my bed.

"I thought you hated me," I said choking back a sob.

He looked revolted at the thought. "I could never hate you."

"Then why were you so mean?"

"I was jealous; I thought you didn't want me. Every time I wanted to talk to you, you sent me away. When I saw you with Chris today I lost it."

"Why would I pick anyone over you?"

"I don't know, girls make no sense," he laughed.

"Well, it will always be you, no matter what." I held his hands in mine.

That's good to know," he said bending over to kiss me.

"Wait," I said stopping him, before he could start and

releasing his hands

"What?"

"What's your problem with Chris?" I asked.

"Nothing," he said, but he knew I didn't believe him.

"Erik, tell me!" Now, this sounded familiar.

"Fine," he said sighing. "I think Chris killed you."

"What! No way! You are so wrong." I definitely couldn't tell him that I had been sleeping on Chris' couch all day, or that he gave me his freakin car.

"Iz, listen to me."

"No."

"I don't want you to see him."

"Excuse me," I said cutting him off.

"Uh, let me finish."

"Please, go on," I said sarcastically.

"I don't want you to see him until I know for sure he didn't kill you."

"I don't care; I'll do what I want. You don't know anything for sure, and I don't believe it. I will see him when I feel like it."

"Fine, it's your life not mine."

"If you're that concerned then change me. Make me like you and then you don't have to worry."

"No way Isabelle. Absolutely not. Not out of fear. When you are really ready. I want to spend forever with you but not like this." He said brushing my hair out of my eyes.

"Fine."

"You can still see him, since I know I cannot stop you. But, you can't be alone with him."

"Whatever."

"I am serious, now go back to sleep, you need it."

"Stay with me Erik." I said with my eyes fixed on his.

"I don't think it's a good idea Iz."

"Please, I am sad; I'm missing my dad a lot."

"All right, for a little bit," he said getting next to me in bed.

"Promise me you'll be here when I wake up."

"Okay, I promise."

Chapter 19: War

"Katherine, Katherine, I need to talk to you." James came running to me as I was collecting eggs in a basket for our breakfast. He sounded frantic.

"The news around town is that a war broke out, the Confederate army attacked Fort Sumter. Lincoln is calling for a voluntary army from each state."

"Oh my God what does this mean?" I dropped the basket of eggs on the ground.

"Katherine, our breakfast," James complained.

"Go on," I said wiping the tears.

"The Mayor is having a meeting at his house tonight to recruit men. I'm going to go. I want to join the Union Army."

I starting cleaning up and gathering the eggs that weren't broken. "No James, why would you join an army? Why can't they just send Nathan? Nobody will miss him while

Flashback

he's gone."

James laughed, "I bet you're right, but I'm going to do this. There's no way you're going to stop me."

I tried to argue with him more, but he just wouldn't listen. He was stubborn, just like me.

We went to the kitchen to make breakfast. My father and Daniel were at the kitchen table talking about the attack on Fort Sumter. There was a knock at the back door.

"I'll get it," I said rushing to the door.

It was Erik. I tried not to show any emotion toward him in front of my dad.

"By your faces I could tell you've all heard the news," Erik said coming in.

"I am ready to go, friend," Daniel said.

"You guys are all loony," I said trying not to get upset.

"Katherine, we have to go, do you want to end up like those innocent people in Fort Sumter?" My dad said getting up from the table and walking out the door. Daniel followed. Kiss up.

"Are you planning to go too?" I asked Erik as soon as they left.

"Yes, I am Katherine. Why does it matter, you're still engaged to Nathan."

"Yeah, what are we going to do about that?" James

asked.

"Stop trying to change the subject," I said. "It matters," I said turning to Erik, "I love you, not him."

"Can we go outside and talk about this?" Erik asked.

He took my hand and led me out the back-door and into the field. We sat on the dew-covered grass and held each other's hands. I put my head on his shoulder and looked down at the grass. He put his hand under my chin and lifted my head up turning me towards him.

"I'm going to be fine, don't worry. Your brothers will be too. This is just something we have to do."

"Don't try to make me feel better. I don't want you to go. Don't leave me."

"You won't be alone for long, you'll be with Nathan soon," he said sadly.

"But I don't want to be with him, I am trying to figure something out. A way to be with you. Maybe we can prove to my father that I will be better off with you," I said getting choked up.

"I don't live in a mansion and I cannot offer you everything Nathan can. But I will sure try."

"I don't need a mansion. I don't care about any of it. I just want you," I said cheering up at the thought.

"But that is what your father wants for you. I cannot

come between you two."

"But you can. Don't go to war. Run away with me the day of my wedding. Nathan won't know what to do."

"Katherine, I love you, but I am not sure that I can take you from your family." He stroked the back of my neck trying to soothe me.

"If you will not be with me, you will leave me miserable for the rest of my life."

"At least I can make you happy in this moment," he said pressing his lips into mine.

I kissed him and thought about running away at that very minute.

"I want to be happy forever Erik, not just right now." I sighed.

"I know Katherine; I promise we will live in bliss."

Chapter 20: Together

I woke up sad. Not knowing if Erik ever really went to war or not. I rolled over in bed and felt that it was empty.

"Erik?" That's nice, promise me something, and then leave. Awesome.

"What?" he asked coming through the door.

"You know that is abandonment."

"I went to Dunkin Donuts to get you a Hazelnut ice coffee, your favorite."

"Abandonment," I said laughing and ignoring that he had done something sweet for me.

"You're not funny Isabelle, that was not abandonment," he said not laughing.

"Whatever you say. You abandoned me in my room," I said under my breath.

"I am not fighting with you about abandonment; I will show you abandonment so you can learn the definition."

Flashback

I giggled, pulling him towards me. "Show me," I whispered.

"I would never abandon you."

"I love you."

"I love you too," he said kissing me.

"Iz, wake up," Jocelyn said coming in the room.

She stopped dead in her tracks as Erik and I pulled away from each other. "When, when, when did he get here?" She stuttered.

She seemed to get the picture and said, "Oh my God, he slept here over night?"

We nodded our heads.

She rolled her eyes and turned around toward the door.

"Just hurry up and get ready for school."

"That was awkward," I laughed.

"Yeah it was. Now go, go make yourself pretty, you look like Raggedy Ann."

I laughed and said, "Yes sir," as I saluted him.

I went into the bathroom to get changed and do my hair. "How do I look?" I asked walking back into my bedroom.

"Beautiful," he said kissing me. "As always."

"Now that was worth getting myself all dolled up," I said pulling away.

"Definitely," he said laughing. "We have to get to school."

"Awww, do we have to?"

"Yes!"

"Why?" I moaned.

"Because I want to go to school."

"Since when do you like school?" I questioned.
"Nobody, and I mean nobody, not even the nerds like school."

"Since I get to be with you during classes."

"Not every class," I pointed out.

"True," he said shrugging.

"Fine, but I am driving."

"Whatever you want love."

"I wanna go to Connecticut."

I can't believe I blurted that out. I've wanted to go to Connecticut for years. I wanted to see my home, my town. And since he said, "whatever you want." That is what I wanted at that moment. That is what I was thinking about. The two of us could go see it together.

"What?" He asked taken aback.

"Nothing."

"Tell me."

"Just drop it."

Just then I got a text. It was from an unknown sender:

Be careful who you trust. The ones you love could be lying to you.

What was that supposed to mean? Was it about Erik? He must have seen the terrified look on my face because he asked if I was okay.

"Yeah, I'm fine," I said.

"You can tell me anything, Iz."

"Yeah I know."

"Good," he said as we walked outside to the car.

"Why is Chris' car parked here?"

"Because it is mine now."

"Are you freakin' kidding me, he gave you car. For what reason?"

"Uh, because I needed one. Just get in the damn car. I am not talking about this."

When we got in the car I got another text. It was from Chris.

Meet me at school.

Sure, at the front gate? I text back.

Kay, see you there.

"Who was that?"

"Chris."

"And now he's texting you." He said exasperated.

"Be nice, he's my friend."

"He seems to like you more than that. He gave you a freakin' car. I could have done that."

"It's just a car, relax. Are we going to talk about this the whole ride to school?"

"Just a car my ass. He probably thinks it's an engagement present. I bet there is a ring in the glove compartment. Damn, he beat me to it." Erik said sarcastically, opening the glove box.

"Not funny."

"You're right, because I'm serious."

"You know I love you, not him." Or at least I don't think I love Chris?

"That makes me feel a lot better." He rolled his eyes.

"Hey I kind of remember how back then you wanted to go fight in a war. Did you ever go?" I asked changing the subject.

"Yeah, I did, I fought in the Civil War."

"Oh my God you did," I was shocked.

"I was devastated after you died. I left a couple of days after your funeral and joined the army."

"That's incredible Erik, what was it like?" I wondered.

"Like a horrible war, which I couldn't wait to end. I

knew I couldn't die, but I had to watch my friends get killed."

"You must have been so sad."

"I was, but knowing that me being there saved many people made me want to fight more."

He paused for a minute. I didn't know what else to say. I couldn't picture him fighting.

"It's funny sitting in History class listening to the teacher telling us what happened, when I know the truth and I can picture it the right way. I fought under Ulysses S. Grant, Iz, one of the most famous men in history and I can't tell anyone. I was with him for two years and helped to siege Petersburg, taking down Lee's army."

Wow. I thought my life was hard. He has all this powerful information and he really can't share it with anyone. I just have my stupid dreams all to myself.

"I try not to think about it much. It is a part of History, but it was the worst war of all time, we lost more people than any other war to date, about 600,000 lives."

"That must have been so hard for you to watch."

"I couldn't bring myself to participate in another war. So, I never did," he said sadly.

"Well, I am sure you accomplished many wonderful things in the past hundred years. I would love to hear all about them. Then I could just skip History from now on," I

Flashback

said laughing, trying to put him in a better mood.

We were finally at school and Chris was waiting for me at the gate. I parked the car and we got out. "Hey Chris," I said hugging him. I could feel Erik and Chris staring each other down while we were hugging.

"Hey, beautiful," Chris said releasing me.

Beautiful! So what if Chris is just my friend, he can call me beautiful right?

Erik growled and put his arm around me.

"What's up?" I asked as we all walked toward the building.

"Same old, same old, you?" Chris replied.

"We're thinking about going to Connecticut for spring break. But we're not sure yet even though she really wants to," Erik said.

Why would he say that? I shot him a look.

"Why would you say that?" I sent the thought to him.

"Because I did," he sent back.

"Awesome," Chris said as we walked into school.

The second bell rang. "Uh we gotta get to class, we missed homeroom again," I said.

"I'll walk you," Erik said.

"It's okay, I can walk her. You don't have first period near us. I wouldn't want you to have to walk all the way to her class and back."

"Whatever," Erik said walking away.

"Why did you do that Chris?"

"Do what?"

"He wanted to walk with me."

"I know."

"So, then why did you do it?"

"I really, really like you Isabelle."

I am so blind! "Oh."

"What I want to know is do you like me too?"

"I...I don't know." I was completely caught off guard.

"It's okay, think about it."

"Ummm...Ok let's get to class."

"Yeah."

When we got to class Mr. Simmons was writing some math equations, I didn't understand on the board.

"Ms. Halloway, Mr. Smython, do you have a reason for being late for class?"

His name is Smython? Where did I hear that name before? Christopher Smython. Feels like déjà vu.

"We just, uh."

"Her sister's in the hospital. We came here to tell you we won't be here for the day."

What? I can't believe he just said that. Maybe he is a

liar, maybe I can't trust him.

Mr. Simmons's face softened, "I'm so sorry Ms. Halloway, between her and your father, um I don't know what to say. Get there safe and please contact me if you need anything."

"Ummm, okay," I stuttered and walked out of the room following Chris. Our classmates just stared in awe.

When we got outside I yelled at Chris, "Why the hell would you do that? Are you freakin insane?"

"Maybe, but uh check your phone."

What? Why would I check my phone? But I did anyway. I had two missed calls from my mom and two text messages. One from my mom and the other from Evelyn. I forgot she's in Mr. Simmons class. The message from my mom read:

> *Your sister is at St. Vincent's hospital, I called*
> *the school. Come meet me as soon as you can.*

Oh my God I guess Chris was right. The message from Evelyn said:

> *Your sister is in the hospital? Should I get*
> *excused from class and come with you?*

I replied:

Flashback

No, it's fine. I can handle it. Just don't tell

anyone yet, not even Erik.

I didn't want Erik to come rushing to my aid, or getting mad that I was with Chris. It would be best if he didn't find out right now.

Okay, she text back.

"You were right," I said to Chris. But how did he know? How did he find out before me? This was getting strange.

"I know, now get in the car, I'm driving."

Chapter 21: Hospital

When we got to the hospital my mom was in the waiting room. She got up and threw her arms around me. "Oh honey, I'm so glad you're here. Your sister was in an accident. The doctor let me go in and see her. She was alert but they are still running some tests. Is this Erik?"

"No, this is Chris."

"Oh, the just friend one." She smirked.

"Uh, yeah," I said looking embarrassed.

"Nice to meet you Mrs. Halloway," Chris said as he put his hand out.

My mom shook his hand and said, "And you as well, please call me Emily."

"Okay, Emily." Chris smiled.

"Thank you Chris for coming to support my daughter."

"You're welcome."

Flashback

"I'm sure you would like to come see your sister now," my mom said looking at me with sad eyes.

"Yes, but do you mind if I talk to her alone?"

"Not at all, she's in room B30," my mom said.

"Thanks," I said as I walked away.

I hate hospitals. They all have an unusual smell. It is like a clean odor mixed with the scent of death. The walls are so bare. Maybe a splash of color would help make it look not so psycho-wardish.

As I walked down the long narrow hall I got a text message from the same unknown sender:

First I'll hurt the ones you love.
Then you're next.

Who is this person? Why does everyone around me have to get hurt? Why can't he just come for me? I'm not that special. But the voice in the back of my head told me different. I replied to the message:

Leave me and my family alone.

He replied:

I will come for you.

My hands shaking, I responded:

Then come. Just leave them alone and take
me.

My phone buzzed back immediately:

No, I want you to see what pain is.
Meet me in the alley behind Angelo's
Restaurant at midnight.

Should I say yes? My gut told me absolutely not. But this could be my chance to see who killed me.

I'll be there.

I continued to walk down the hallway and into my sister's room. When I opened the door and she saw me, her face lit up. But she looked horrible. She had a cast on her right leg and on her left arm. There was bloody gauze wrapped around her head. My stomach knotted up. Could this have happened to her because of me?

"Jocelyn, I am so sorry. Are you okay?" I asked.

"I've been better," she said with a half-hearted smile.

"What happened?"

"I have a broken leg, a broken arm and a concussion. I had to get a few stitches."

"No, I mean how did it happen?" I questioned.

"Oh well, I got into a car accident."

"What caused it?"

"I saw something move in front of my car on the highway. I just reacted and swerved. But I hit two other cars."

"Was it an animal?"

"No, it looked like a human but I'm not really sure it was. It moved with incredible speed and looked like a blur when it ran. The doctor said I was hallucinating, maybe a side effect from my migraine medicine."

"Did you see its face?"

"No, it was too fast."

I was about to ask another question when she said, "What's with all the questions? Could we not talk about this?"

"All right." I sighed.

I really wanted to get as much information out of her as possible, but I didn't want to push her when I knew she was hurt. That's all I could get her to talk about at the time.

"You don't have to stay Iz, I'm okay. But can you get mom for me?"

"Okay, I'll go get her, I love you Joc."

Good. I can go home. I needed to have some time to make sense of all the things that had happened. Maybe I could think more clearly at my house. I left the room and went to tell my mom that Jocelyn needed her.

Flashback

Chapter 22: Uhh, Men

Chris dropped me home and I went inside. I grabbed some peanut butter crackers and ran up to my room. When I opened the door I saw Erik sitting on my bed.

"Are you okay? I heard about what happened," he said.

So, Evelyn did tell him after I specifically asked her not to!

"Yeah I'm okay."

"And I see your *buddy* Chris brought you home. The bastard actually tried to do something nice for once," he smirked.

"For once? He gave me a freakin' car."

"Almost forgot, brought your car here."

"You hijacked my car?" I asked holding up the keys.

"Yes, I did, is that a problem?" He asked.

"No, I think it's hot," I said leaning over the bed to kiss him.

"Well, I'm glad you think that. I'll have to do it more often," he laughed.

"Definitely," I laughed back. "Kiss me again."

"Are you sure you don't want to kiss Chris instead?"

"Don't be stupid." I said and kissed him again.

The door swung open.

"Uhh, Uhh I'm sorry. I knocked at the door and no one answered. I got nervous and came in I'll leave you two love birds alone," Chris said sarcastically.

"It's okay, what do you need?" I asked.

Ignoring me he said, "Does she know?"

"Know what?" Erik replied, making the 'you better shut up' face.

Why are they talking about me? I am right in front of them. Hello? "Ummmm I'm right here ya know. What don't I know?"

"Nothing," they said in unison.

"Well, what is he talking about Erik?" I questioned.

"Don't worry about that right now Isabelle."

"Whatever, I'll find out myself," I said under my breath.

"Okay, nice being here and all but I got to go," Chris

said sarcastically. "I just came here to give you your backpack."

"Thanks," I said rolling my eyes because I was annoyed at the both of them.

"Bye," he said walking out the door.

"Actually, I gotta go too," Erik said after Chris left!

"Uhh, see ya," I said gladly as he left too.

I went over to the window and watched them drive away. I was glad they left. It was already getting late and I needed time to think before I met the anonymous caller behind the restaurant.

Flashback

Chapter 23: Meeting

It was finally midnight. I grabbed a jacket but threw my phone on my bed and left it home. I drove really slow to Angelo's contemplating whether or not to turn around. When I got to the alley no one was there. It was pitch black. It didn't matter that all the streetlights were on.

I stood in the middle of the alley in between all of the dumpsters and boxes from the surrounding businesses. A figure walked towards me as if he came out of nowhere. My heart began to race. I could tell it was a man by the way he walked and his body was built. He was wearing a black hoodie and jeans. I couldn't make out his face.

"You're here," he said in a deep voice, his lips curling into a smile. His voice sounded familiar. Was it Erik? Impossible. I can't believe the thought even crossed my mind. Could it be Chris? He couldn't do that, could he?

"Yes, I am. Now what do you want?" I asked.

"You, it's always you," he said coming closer, whispering in my ear. His hot breath brought back the memory of the night of the mayor's ball. Nathan? I wondered. It couldn't be, he's dead. He held my body against him and squeezed my arm.

"Then kill me already."

"All in good time, I want you to feel what real pain is. Physical and emotional. First your family and then I'll come for you," he said pressing a knife against my arm cutting through my purple striped shirt.

"Ouch," I screamed. Damn it that hurt.

"Oh, does that hurt? Sorry!" he said flinging me into the brick wall.

My head hit the wall with a loud bang and I fell to the ground.

"You're a real bastard, you know that?" I yelled, holding the top of my head, feeling quite dizzy.

"Get it all the time."

I tried to get up and winced.

"Don't worry I won't kill you, yet," he laughed.

"Why is that again?" I asked sarcastically.

Sighing he said, "I am not one to explain things twice but I'll give you more time to experience love, and more pain."

"Just do it now." I grinded my teeth as I lay on the ground still too weak to get up.

"Begging will get you nowhere," he said digging his nails into the back of my neck. He was holding my head up now, close to his face.

I flinched, "Who are you?"

"That's for me to know and you to find out." Then like the bastard he is he slammed my head against the brick wall again. I fell to the ground unconscious.

"Don't you dare touch her again," Erik ran towards him, realizing he was too late.

"Relax," the man said standing over my limp body.

"Do not tell me to relax. My girlfriend is lying on the ground, bleeding, unconscious and almost dead. "Isabelle wake up." He said leaping towards the man.

"Like I said I won't kill her yet," he said as he threw Erik against the wall with so much force a few bricks fell out. He darted down the alley. The man was gone by the time Erik got up.

*

Thirty minutes later I woke up on my bed with Erik by my side watching over me. I felt sore but all my injuries were gone. How the hell did that happen?

"You're up," Erik said flatly.

"No really?"

"Why do you always have to be so sarcastic? You scared the hell out of me. What were you thinking going to meet that wacko alone? Are you on a suicide mission or something?"

"No, I wanted to find out who my killer is."

"And, we will, eventually, but you getting killed wouldn't have gotten our answer any sooner Iz."

"Whatever, but how are all my injuries gone?"

"I don't know," he smiled secretively.

"Yeah right, what else are you hiding from me? Oh and I thought you hated Chris, and now you two are keeping secrets from me."

"I'll tell you what we were talking about if that makes you happy."

"You better," I said making a fist.

"He's a vampire." Well I should've seen that coming. Shows how smart I am.

"He asked if you know what we are. I told him no. I didn't want him to know you knew. He may be your friend, but I sure as hell hate him."

"Okay," was all I said. I didn't think that's the only thing he's hiding from me. There's definitely more.

"What did he say?" Erik asked.

"Who, Chris?"

"No, your killer."

"Speaking of killer how'd you know where to find me?"

"Isabelle, don't change the subject."

"Well, I really want to know how you found me, since I block you from all my thoughts now."

"Fine," Erik sighed, "I read your texts."

"You what!" I yelled. Okay stalker! I don't care if he is my boyfriend. That was an invasion of privacy.

"What did you think I was going to leave you unprotected? And yeah you won't let me into your head so I had to do something. I'm not a jerk. End of subject. Now tell me what he said."

"He, he said that he'd give me more time to experience love and what real pain feels like."

"That's messed up. What else did he say?"

"That he'd hurt the ones I love and then come for me. Erik I'm scared."

"Isabelle, listen to me. He won't kill your family, and

don't worry about your friends."

"He killed my father Erik, and he will kill me," I cried.

"I know, I know," he said cradling me in his arms. "But I will protect you; I will stop at nothing to protect you. I got to the alley too late, put I promise that will never happen again."

"Erik, he will kill me, just like he did before." I sobbed with my hands covering my eyes.

"No he won't. Don't you ever say that. I will never let that happen," he said trying to console me as he rubbed my back.

"But how do you know for sure?"

"Because I can't live without you again."

"As long as we're telling each other the truth, I need to tell you something." Well at least I am telling the truth, I know he was hiding something.

"What Iz?"

"Sometimes when I go to sleep or pass out I have these dreams about my past. How I met you, how I died. They scare me Erik. It, it feels like things from our past our happening again, but differently. You hide things from me, we fight, I cry, we make up. I was also threatened in both lives and hurt. The killer reminds me of Nathan. Could it be Nathan?" I rambled on.

"It's okay Iz, I hope all your dreams aren't bad. Don't

you have any happy memories of us? Maybe it is Nathan, but I still think it's that scumbag Chris."

"Of course I have great memories too, I just can't remember everything. It's hard to put it all together sometimes. Anyway, give me one good reason why you think it's Chris."

"Do you hear the way he speaks to you?"

"Yeah, if you mean kindly, I don't understand. Any other reasons you would like to share?"

"Never mind," he sighed.

"See, exactly you have no good reasons, you just hate him." I pouted

"Well you can't be sure that it wasn't him under that hood. You didn't see anything right?" He put his hand under my chin to look me in the eye.

"No, I didn't."

"So, you can't say I am completely wrong because you do not know the truth."

"True, but I still say he's not. Why don't we just ask him? It would be easier."

"Sure, Isabelle we will just ask the person who could be your killer if he really is. That's not baiting yourself or anything," he said sarcastically.

"Well, it's not him so we don't have to."

"Well if it wasn't him why wasn't he there to save you like I did?"

"I'm not fighting with you about this Erik. There is a dangerous killer out there."

"Fine, I don't want to argue."

"Wait, what time is it? Where is my mom?"

"It's like 1:30 A.M., you should go to bed. I saw a note from your mom on the kitchen table that she is sleeping at the hospital with your sister."

"Stay with me again, I don't want to be alone," I said rubbing my hand up and down his smooth, strong forearm.

"I wasn't going to leave anyways, not after what happened," Erik said softly, putting his other arm around me.

"Good, maybe I can get some sleep with you here." I moved to the other side of the bed giving him room to lie next to me.

"Goodnight Isabelle, I love you," he said, pulling my fluffy purple blanket over us and tucking me in.

"I love you too Erik, until death." I had to add that last part because I knew I was going to die no matter what he says.

"You won't have to worry about the death part," he said.

Chapter 24: The Next Day

"**Erik**," I asked groggily as I rubbed my eyes then felt the other side of my bed.

"I'm here," he muttered coming into my bedroom.

"Oh good! I thought you left again."

"You don't have to worry about that, I will never leave you."

Great. Now that blows my plans to figure things out on my own.

"I'm sorry, all the time?"

"Yes, and that means you will not go to Chris' house today after school to talk."

"What?" I yelled, sitting straight up in my bed. I have no idea what the hell he is talking about.

"Chris texted you to see if you want to go over. He

wants to talk to you."

"You read my text again!" Not that I talk about anything worthwhile reading. But seriously, why does he keep reading my texts?

"Yeah, is it a problem?"

"I guess not. But are you going to be one of those psycho boyfriends that reads my texts and goes through my emails and things? Are you going to be the crazy jealous type? Because that's not gonna work for me. Except the jealous thing because that's hot on you." I said sarcastically. I thought if I made him laugh he wouldn't care if I went to Chris'.

He laughed, "Very funny, but you're still not going to see Chris without me."

"What, you're being ridiculous," I said annoyed.

"No, I'm not, would you like to die? Be my guest."

"Come on be reasonable. If you are going to come with me, you have to stay outside in the car."

"Fine, but if I sense that there's something wrong I'm coming in."

"Good, then it's a deal?" I smirked.

"It's a deal. I thought you'd see it my way," he laughed. "We better hurry up or we'll be late for school."

*

We went to school and practiced for the play. At lunch Erik kept saying things about Chris, and it was really tiring to hear him harp on it. He said he thought Chris didn't come to school because he was planning to kill me! How stupid is he? Like always I didn't have any homework. I do it all in class when we have extra time (we always have extra time). After school we went to Chris' house.

We pulled up to Chris' big white colonial house. It had maroon trim and shutters. Chris did all the landscaping in the front yard. He is so meticulous that his house looks like it belonged on Wisteria Lane. It almost looks like Nathan's mansion, but smaller. He can't be Nathan, he is a vampire and looks nothing like him. But I am starting to think Erik could be right. I need to get to the bottom of all this once and for all.

"Don't pull in the driveway Erik," I said. "Just park on the side of the road. Try to stay out of sight please."

"Okay. But don't forget if I think there is something wrong I am coming in."

"Fine, if I feel like I am in danger I will open my mind to you, but everything is going to be fine," I said. At least I know he's here to protect me if he ends up being right.

I got out of the car and walked up the stone pathway.

I rang the bell.

"Hey," Chris said as he let me in.

Flashback

I had been in his house before but now I started analyzing everything about it. From the hardwood floors to the paintings on the wall. It was decorated similarly to Nathan's mansion but more contemporary.

He had some nice furniture but I really didn't like the brown couches.

"Hi, what is it that you want to tell me?" Somebody had to start the conversation. I wasn't going to just stand there in awkward silence until somebody said something.

"Everything."

Are you kidding me? Now he's starting to sound like Erik with his 'everything.' What's with vampires these days? They have to say everything when they're just going to tell you something. What the hell is everything? For all I know it could be everything about him from sixth grade to seventh grade or from 1800 to 2011.

"What is everything supposed to mean?" I inquired.

"Well, I will start with this, I am a vampire," he said seriously.

Was I supposed to play dumb or just tell him I know? I blurted out, "I know that!"

He looked surprised. "What? How do you know?"

"Erik told me. I already knew about him and then I figured out you were one, too," I said, even though I really didn't want to sell out Erik.

"Then if you know that, then you must know who I am."

Was this another trick question? Was he going to admit he's Nathan? "Yeah, you're Chris, I know that."

"Then you don't know," he sighed. "I can't believe you don't remember your own best friend."

Now he's really confusing me. "What the heck are you talking about?"

"I don't know if I should tell you now."

"Uh, yes," I said rolling my eyes.

"Oh Isabelle, he said holding my hands in his, "in your old life I was your best friend. But once you met Erik I was always in the shadows. We did everything together. I loved you then and I still love you now. I was envious when you met Erik. The night of the ball we were supposed to go together even though you were betrothed to Nathan. I was going to tell you how I felt that night, but I couldn't find you. I found you later dancing with Erik. When I saw you kiss him, I was completely broken. There was never another moment to tell you."

As he spoke I began to remember. He was my best friend, Christopher. Why didn't' Erik tell me and why haven't I dreamt about him before? He was right; we really did do everything together. We rode my horses, he helped me with my chores, and we went to the market together, played in the field, and looked at the clouds in the day and the stars at night. It all came back to me. There wasn't a moment when he wasn't at my side until I met Erik. He even asked me to run away with him. Run away from all things I didn't want my life to be. Be free. That was our aspiration. "I, I remember!" I screeched. "You asked me to run away with you once. But I didn't know it was because you loved me that way. I thought it was because you knew I despised Nathan. You didn't want to be a farmer like your father. Our dream was to get away from everything we didn't want."

"It was our dream Iz, all the things you mentioned," he whispered.

"I'm sorry I must have been totally clueless."

"It's okay," he said, and then he added, "Kiss me."

He is crazy. Why would I do that? He's one of my best friends and I have a boyfriend. But before I could answer, he was already kissing me. It was amazingly amazing. His lips were warm and soft. But I knew I had to pull away. It wasn't fair to Erik.

I pulled away and screamed, "Why would you do that? Are you freakin' crazy?"

Of course Erik came rushing in through the front door.

Flashback

He sensed I was nervous. "What is it? Are you okay?" Erik asked.

"I'm fine, Chris just kissed me." Maybe I shouldn't have said that.

"You kissed your murderer! What the hell is wrong with you?"

"For the record he's not my murderer, and there's nothing wrong with me," I said getting really mad.

"She's right. And as long as I'm this far, I really think she should pick me," Chris said.

"And why is that?" Erik growled.

"Well I'm not the one hiding things from her," Chris snapped back.

Hiding things from me? Ahah! I knew he was hiding something.

"What's he hiding from me?" I inquired.

"Would you like to tell her Erik, or should I?" Chris said with a devilish look in his eye.

Erik was totally speechless. His chin seemed to tremble. He just looked at me then at Chris and back at me without saying a word.

"Okay, then I will. He turned your brothers Isabelle. They are still alive. Oh and while we're at it I will tell you something you didn't know about yourself. You are *special*

Isabelle; there is something different about you. You're human, but you're more than that. That is why your mother died in the past. Who knows why Emily didn't, but maybe you will find out when you learn more about yourself. I guess that's enough of humiliating Erik for now."

Oh my God, my brothers are alive? I'm special, what the heck is he talking about? I don't feel special, most of the time I feel like a loser. None of this makes sense. Can my life get any weirder? "Erik, how could you do that?" I questioned angrily. My head frowned, my eyes teared.

"Isabelle, I am so sorry, I did it before I met you. I was young and stupid. I was alone and needed company."

"So, you turned my brothers because you wanted friends forever, awesome," I said pissed.

"Then they introduced me to you and everything changed. James thought it would be a good idea if one of us turned you and then we could all be together. I was going to turn you the night before you were to marry Nathan, but you died before I could. We were all so devastated that you died, it tore us apart. We all went our separate ways. I couldn't stand being with them. They reminded me of you, especially James."

"This is all so much to take in right now. But I do want to know if you are still in touch with them?"

"I'm not Isabelle, I'm sorry, please forgive me," he pleaded.

"I am," Chris said.

"Both of them?" I said excited.

"About that, I don't know how you'll take this, but James is here. We are trying to track down Daniel," Chris responded.

"James is here! Where is he? I want to see him."

"Upstairs, I can get him if you want."

"Of course she wants me dumbass, I'm just that great."

My head whipped around. That could only be one person or vampire. "James!" I exclaimed running into his arms.

"Oh Katherine, how I've missed you." He sighed as he wrapped his muscular arms around me. His eyes looked me up and down as if he wanted to capture my new essence in his mind.

Hearing the sound of his voice was one of the best things that ever happened to me, I couldn't help but cry. Even though he sounded like someone from a bad romance movie.

"Kay, why are you crying?" He called me Katherine and used my nickname. Doesn't he know I have a different name? I look completely different; I am not the same girl anymore.

"I just missed you, and I can't believe you're really here. Where's Daniel? No matter how miserable he is, I still miss him." I snickered as I unfolded my body from his tight bear hug.

He held my hands tightly in his, "I'm here, I will protect you Isabelle. I heard about everything. I miss him too; we're trying to locate him. Last I heard from him, he was in Colorado. And by the way, you are still so beautiful even though you look so different."

"I'm not beautiful," I smiled with tears of happiness rolling down my cheeks.

"I can't believe you called me Isabelle and no sarcastic remark about Daniel?"

"I'm saving those for when he comes." He said wiping my tears with his soft hands.

I laughed. "How did you get here?" I asked.

"Chris tracked me down. He said you needed help. Of course I came to help my little sis. I just can't believe you're alive."

"Thanks James, me either. Being reincarnated is a little much," I said with a smile.

If only Daniel could help too. I hoped they would find him.

Flashback

"So, see I can't be her murderer, I'm helping," Chris pointed out interrupting my moment with James.

"Oh really, because I think you are. You could be setting us up and making us think you're helping," Erik said not so nicely. He stared Chris up and down as if he could pounce on him at any moment.

James just shook his head at the both of them and sat on the couch. He leisurely put his Chuck Taylors on the coffee table as if he cared less and was ready to smoke a cigarette.

James is not much for confrontation.

"Well, you're wrong and maybe you're just jealous that I'm closer to her than you'll ever be. She will tell me things Erik that she will never tell you." Chris rolled his big brown eyes. Tension began to fill the air.

"Whatever you say Chris, then let me hear some stories." Erik was getting nasty and his eyes had a hue of black.

"The night before she died Katherine told me she had this vision, it made her pass out like she does now. Did she tell you that Erik?" He threw his hands up in the air. "Well, she told me someone was going to get her. She was afraid. She said she knew she was going to die but didn't know when. I bet she didn't trust you enough to tell you."

"I do to trust him!" I screamed throwing a pillow at

Chris.

He caught it and shushed me. "Let me finish please."

I sat back on the couch and crossed my arms.

"She had seen herself dead already and her visions had never been like that before. I didn't believe her, but obviously after she died I knew it was true. She also saw you before she met you. She kept saying, 'I had this vision about this man that I fell in love with.' It didn't make sense. I kept telling her it was a dream. And that's only some of the things she told me. You think you know her? Well I'll be damned even more than I already am." Chris said angrily.

I became nervous. I did not want them to fight. I looked at Erik to stop this madness but it didn't matter.

"I know her enough. And you think I'm jealous? Let me tell you, I am far from that. If anyone's jealous it's you. At least I have her." Erik yelled, getting closer to Chris, ready to punch him.

I signaled James to break it up. He shrugged his shoulders and leaned back putting his hands behind his head, "Just relax guys come on there are more important things than who knows her better. My sister's life is on the line here," James interrupted.

Relax? Where have I heard that before? Erik noticed too, but everybody, uses relax, right? James wouldn't, I mean he really wouldn't. It's not him.

"Fine," Erik sighed, as he backed away from Chris

"Alright," Chris grunted.

"As long as we're off the fighting thing, isn't it your birthday May 11th, next Saturday, Isabelle? I saw it listed when I found you online. Bet both of you didn't know that. Yeah, you guys know her real well," James said smugly.

"It's your birthday Saturday Iz, that's in a week. Why wouldn't you tell me?" Erik sounded hurt.

It's just a birthday. Plus every year on my birthday something bad happens. Like last year my dog Ellie died. And the year before that I broke my arm while riding my skateboard. The year before that I lost one of my best friends. No, she didn't die; we're just not friends anymore! Her name was Rikki. We got into a big fight and then she moved away before we could make up. Should I go on with the horrible list? I think not.

"Yes, give us some answers," Chris said.

"It's not that big of a deal." Why do they care?

"Yes it is Isabelle, please tell me why you didn't tell us," Erik pleaded.

"You could've asked my friends, they would have told you."

"Isabelle, tell me now," Erik demanded.

That's a good way to get me to tell him. I hate being talked to like a child. I don't have to tell him if I don't want to.

Like Chris read my mind he said, "Like that's the way to get her to tell you. Iz, just please tell us why you didn't let us know it is your birthday."

"Fine. I'll tell you. Every year something bad happens on my birthday. So I tend not to like to celebrate it."

"Well, that's no big deal. And nothing bad can happen with us here. We're having a party for you on Saturday," Chris said grinning.

"No, absolutely not!" I was not happy, I bit my lip.

"Yes we are, come on live a little," James said still chilling on the couch.

I sat down next to James and looked for Erik to help me out but he just shrugged. *Thanks a lot*, I tried to mindspeak to Erik.

"Okay, fine," I said giving in, "But where?"

"Your house of course," Chris said sitting on the other ugly brown couch across from me.

"Then who's coming? I have like no friends." I said stating the obvious.

"Don't say that. We are all your friends. We will be there and I'm sure Evelyn and Rachael will come too," Chris answered.

"We can start planning tomorrow," James said.

Chapter 25: Jocelyn

"I can't believe you let them talk me into have a party for me," I said to Erik when we got to my house.

"I can't believe you didn't tell me your birthday's in eight days." Erik said falling back on the blue loveseat. I sat down next to him.

Right after he said that my front door opened.

"Mom?"

"Yeah, it's me. Your sister won't be out of the hospital until Sunday." She said as she dashed into the living room and then to the kitchen. "They found some internal bleeding. I'm just getting a few things because I'm staying with her at the hospital. I'm sorry I have to run out like this. I won't have time to plan a party for you this week but I will make it up to you. I promise," she said sadly as she frantically gathered

Flashback

things and threw them into her brown Coach overnight bag.

Ignoring what she said about my birthday I asked, "Oh my God is she going to be okay?"

My stomach was in a knot. I didn't want to make my mom nervous by asking too many questions.

"Yes they can help her, don't worry about your sister," she replied tossing a Cosmo magazine into her bag.

From the look on her face I could tell that she was scared. I could see her mascara and eyeliner had been running from all the crying she'd been half trying to hide from me.

"Okay, but tell her I will come visit her tomorrow and please call me later after you talk to the doctor."

"I will, and I will let her know, I am sure she will be happy to see you. Now, are you going to introduce me to your friend?"

"Oh yeah, I'm sorry, this is Erik, mom."

"Nice to meet you Erik, I'm Emily," she said with a big smile on her face. This was the first time I have seen her smile since dad died. I guess she was glad to finally meet the boy that was making me so giddy.

"Well, I'm sorry I cannot stay and chat. I really have to be getting back to the hospital." She looked nervously at Erik.

"Wait mom, I just finished the book *Anew* so you can

take it to her for her to read. Let me run up to my room and get it." I jumped off the couch and ran to my room and took the book out of my bookcase. I am so particular about my books that I have to have them all in alphabetical order by Author so that I can easily find them. I grabbed a yellow sticky note off my desk and stuck it to the book. I wrote a quick note that said, 'You'll be okay Joc. I love you so much. See you tomorrow. You're gonna love this book.'

My mom was still downstairs, probably drilling Erik by now.

"So, Erik where exactly are you from? Iz said you just moved here."

"Well, all over the world actually," he responded. "My parents are both in the military so we moved a lot. I am 18 now so I think I might just settle down here. I really like Cali."

"Wow, you must have had an interesting childhood," she said trying to seem interested. Although I am sure she could have cared less about Erik at that particular moment.

I came down the stairs back into the living room. "Enough interrogating him now mom."

She laughed. "I'm not honey, just wondering why he came to a new high school his senior year." She still seemed eager to leave as she glanced at the front door.

"K, well here's the book for Joc." I reached out and put it on the top of her bag.

"Alright, Iz, I'll call you later from the hospital. Here's twenty bucks if you guys want to order a pizza or something for dinner."

"Thanks, mom," I said hugging her goodbye.

"Bye Erik."

"Bye Mrs. Halloway." Erik yelled out the door, because my mom was already at the car by the time he could respond.

"Well that sucks," I said as I flopped down on the couch.

"What? That your mom can't plan anything for you?" He put my hand in his.

Was he not just listening to the conversation?

"Erik," I said all seriously and scared, "that my sister has internal bleeding."

"Oh that. I know, I was trying to get you to not think about that." He pushed my hair away from my eyes still holding me with his other hand.

"Do you think she will be ok?" I asked Erik as tears welled up in my eyes.

"I'm sure she will be, Jocelyn's strong. Everything will be okay. Don't worry it will all work out. I promise you that."

Flashback

I actually felt pretty confident about what he said. "I believe you."

"And I believe that you believe me," he joked.

I laughed, "You really need to come up with better things that make me laugh," I said sarcastically.

"Awww, I thought you liked my jokes."

"I do, but I like you better."

He stared into my eyes and held both my hands tightly. Every time he touches even my hand, my whole body wants to be consumed by him.

"I love you Isabelle, I don't know how many times I can say that until I find a better word to explain my feelings for you. I have felt like this forever. I don't want to be with anyone else but you. So I need to know who's it going to be, Chris or me?"

My body sunk into the couch, he took me by surprise.

"You Erik. It will always be you. You know that don't you?" I wanted him to trust me.

"Somehow I don't believe that. There's something between you and Chris that we don't have. You love him; I can see it in your eyes. Don't deny it Isabelle."

I don't know what my feelings are for Chris. Do I love him?

"Erik, listen to me. You are my soul mate, my true love." I pleaded. I gazed into his eyes so intently as if to tell him with my mind and soul.

"Yeah but, do you love him too?" His question broke my gaze. I looked down at my feet not wanting to look him in the eye any longer.

Oh my God, I love Chris, but I love Erik more. He will always be the one.

"Yes, I do, but the love I have for you is way different. You are my best friend, you have to know that."

"I thought so, but I really hoped I was wrong, I need to go," he said getting angry and pushing me off of him.

"Erik," I said, "Listen to me! I want to be with you and only you forever. Don't walk away from us, don't walk away from me. What we have is unreal."

I tried to reason with him, but he just didn't listen.

"It's fine I've heard enough." He got up off the couch and starting walking to the front door.

"That's unfair; you're the one who brought it up."

I knew he was hurt. I don't blame him. I would be the same way if I knew the one I loved, loved the person I whole heartedly hated.

"There's really no need to explain," he said as he walked out the door.

Flashback

"Don't walk away, I'm talking to you!" I got off the couch and stomped my feet.

*

I spent the next hour crying. I knew I couldn't just sit there and sulk, so I texted Evelyn.

Hi

Hey what's up?

Can you come over? I'll order us a Chinese.

I knew then that Evelyn thought something was up. Since Erik, we haven't really been hanging out. She is a good friend. I'm glad she wasn't mad at me.

Sure- my usual -be there in 10.

Okay doors open u can just come in.

Flashback

The Chinese food came and I threw the forks and crap on the table for the two of us. Evelyn ran into the house like the roadrunner. "Yum, smells good, what's wrong?" She asked.

We sat down, opened the boxes and I started to tell her about Erik and me.

"Erik and I got into a fight. It was pretty bad this time. I don't know if he will ever forgive me."

"Over what?" She asked shoving a piece of lemon chicken into her mouth.

"He asked me if I love Chris."

"Well, do you?"

I didn't answer her.

"Isabelle, do you, or do you not love Chris?" She waved her chopsticks in the air.

"I..., I do."

"Oh my God, you love two smoking hot guys!" She screeched like a ten year old girl waiting backstage to see Justin Bieber.

"Evelyn, that's not the point. I hurt Erik. Erik is the one I want to be with, not Chris. I really don't think Erik will forgive me."

I scooped a big spoonful of Lo mein onto my plate. I swirled it around with my fork and thought about how much I cared about the both of them. Love is hell (especially when you love vampires and they're all damned). I don't want to love Chris, but it's like he put an evil love spell on me. I know I love Erik in ways I can't explain. He's like Heaven to me. But I feel an indescribable connection with Chris.

"Of course he will, Erik loves you too much to leave you because you love some other guy. He would fight for you, he would die for you. You can tell by the way he looks at you, you are his soul mate. He'll come around." She smiled as she bit into her crunchy egg roll. "BTW this eggroll is delic."

"I hope." I kind of giggled because she was talking with a mouthful of food.

It's true, he is my soul mate. I don't know what I'd do if I couldn't be with him.

"Don't worry Iz," she said supportively.

It was really nice talking to Evelyn. I haven't hung out with her in a while.

"Okay, thanks for your ear."

"I'm not Van Gogh, you're welcome though. As long as we're talking about Chris, are you really having a party next Saturday?"

"Yeah he's throwing one for me here." I sighed as I got up and put our dirty dishes into the sink and ran the water over them.

"Okay, good. Because I already got you a present, and

so did Rachael, it will cheer you up."

"You did? You really didn't have to do that."

"But, we wanted to. And besides, we didn't get you anything last year."

That's right; they didn't because I told them not to. I don't like surprises and I usually don't like getting presents. What's wrong with me? I just like spending time with my family and friends on my birthday, like it's any other day.

"Okay, it better not be expensive."

"It is, it's something you'll really like. I have it in my mom's car right now, because I picked it up today."

She packed up the rest of the Chinese and threw it into the fridge for me.

I laughed, "Why do you have it in your mom's car?"

"I was kind of hoping you'd want to have it right now. I'm really excited to see the look on your face when you open it."

"You are such a dork," I giggled.

"That's why you love me."

"Very true," I laughed.

"So do you want it now or not?"

To make her happy I said "yes." She ran out the door and down the stairs to the van.

When she came inside we went up to my room. She

was holding some kind of stand that holds things and something wrapped in a huge box. "What is it?" I asked.

"You'll see, why don't you open it?" She said handing the gifts to me as I sat on my bed. As soon as she gave me the stand, I knew it was for a guitar. So she must have gotten me a guitar.

"Go on; open it," she urged me.

When I ripped the sparkling, shiny silver wrapping paper off and tore open the box I could see the excitement on Evelyn's face. Amongst the bubble wrap lay a black and blue Gibson Melody Maker vintage electric guitar. I was stoked.

"Oh my God, thank you so much." I got up and placed the guitar on its stand next to my other one.

"I knew it was perfect for you when I saw it. I knew you always wanted an electric since you only have an acoustic, so I got it for you. I'm so glad you like it," she said smiling. "I saved all my babysitting money to get it for you."

"Like it? Love it! You didn't have to do that!" I said as I picked the new guitar up again, and grabbed my favorite purple pic off my desk. I started to play and sing Halloween by Dave Matthews, which I thought was appropriate for the way I was feeling after my last encounter with Erik.

"Awesome!" She shouted. "I..."

Just then her phone rang. She frantically waved her

arms at me; apparently there was something she wanted to hear more than my music. I was suddenly cut off from playing my emotional jam.

She talked on her cell for about a minute and then hung up. "I have to go, that was my mom and she needs her car."

Really, she shut my concert down because of her mom? Highly doubtful, she never listens to her mother. It had to be someone else. Didn't my dad text somebody to contact Evelyn? I have to get to the bottom of this.

"Okay," I said just happy to have spent some time with her.

"Bye, I'll try to come see you tomorrow." She hugged me goodbye.

"Bye, thanks Ev."

I really wanted to call Erik but I knew he was still mad at me. I laid in my bed and opened my mind. I hoped he could feel me.

Chapter 26: Dreams

"**Have** you talked to Erik since Friday?" Christopher asked.

"No, he's been distant lately. I saw him in the market this morning and he didn't even say hello," I murmured.

"I'm sure its fine; he'll come around, "Lillian said.

Christopher, Lillian, and I have been best friends since I could remember. Christopher and I met three years ago, and Lillian and I have known each other since we were infants. We tell each other everything. She is going to be one of the witnesses at my wedding if I must go through with it.

"Are you sure Lily?" I asked.

"I'm positive," she said, her green eyes looking me right in the eye, until strands of her strawberry blonde hair draped in front of her eyes.

"But I think he's hiding something from me!" I

Flashback

exclaimed waving my hands in the air.

"Aren't we all Katherine?" Christopher said.

Lillian and I turned to him.

"What is that supposed to mean?" Lillian asked.

Lily's scared he's hiding something from us I thought. She doesn't want her love to be hiding anything. She's wanted him to court her for awhile now, but Christopher doesn't know. She's been working up the nerve to tell him.

"Yes Christopher, what exactly does that mean? Are you hiding something? Feel free to tell us," I said.

"I am hiding nothing of your concern Katherine. Besides, why is this conversation focused on me now? I thought we were talking about Erik."

"We were talking about Erik until you firmly stated that everyone hides things," Lillian gasped.

"Well then, let's go back to talking about Erik, or Nathan."

Why would he just mention Nathan?

"Yes, let's talk about Nathan. What are you going to do about Erik when you marry Nathan?" Lily asked.

"You are getting married in two weeks," Chris said.

"I would rather die than marry that pig," I spat.

"Katherine, don't talk like that," Chris said disturbed.

"Yeah," Lillian chimed in, "we wouldn't want to lose

you."

"I know, it's just that I can't tolerate him. How am I
ever going to marry him?"

"You don't have to. Run away with me. Run away
from all this. Be free. That is our dream. Just me, you and
Lillian. We're perfect together." He grabbed mine and Lillian's
hands trying to twirl us around.

"I don't know Chris," I said sighing. "Why don't you
just go with Lillian?" Of course Lillian wouldn't have minded,
she would've done anything to spend her life with
Christopher. She would've risked everything for him. She
loved him.

"Because I can't!" He exclaimed. "Will you at least
think about it?"

I turned to Lillian taken aback. "No Chris. I can't, I
have a duty to marry him. No matter how much I despise him.
I have to, I'm sorry." I didn't want them to know I really
wanted to run away with Erik. Should I tell them to come
along? Or would they just tell my father.

"Fine," he said exasperatedly, letting go of our hands.
"But will you at least trust me on what I say next?"

I nodded my head.

"Your life depends on it. Something bad will happen.
And no, I don't mean marrying Nathan. Worse."

I stood there shocked he just said that. What could be worse than marrying Nathan? I didn't believe him, he's lying. He just said that to get me to go with him.

"Well I have to go." Lillian said quickly like she knew something she didn't want me to find out. "My mother wants to teach me how to crochet. We all know how that's going to end," she said laughing, "Well goodbye," she swiftly walked away.

When she left, I asked Chris, "What are you hiding?"

"That's for me to know and for you to find out," He said walking away as well.

*

I woke up thinking who was that girl? I had never seen her in my flashbacks before. She didn't look familiar to me. How was I best friends with her? The flashbacks must mean something. All of them do. I only see important things of my past. What was her name again? Lillian. I wondered if she was reincarnated too, or was a vampire? Could she be Evelyn or Rachael? Wait strawberry blonde hair, green eyes. Rachael doesn't have any of those things, but Evelyn does. She also dyes her hair blonde! Although that's not her natural color, strawberry blonde is! So, do I really already know Evelyn? But I can't just go up to her and say it, "Hey Evelyn? I've been meaning to ask you this, did you reincarnate with me?" Um, not going to happen. Although, maybe she knows already, but just hasn't said anything. I mean I didn't know until now.

Questions rambled on in my head so I didn't realize the time. I glanced over at my clock, and it said 11:00 A.M. I had overslept. I wanted to get to the hospital early to see Jocelyn. I quickly went downstairs and made myself breakfast. By breakfast, I mean a bowl of frosted flakes. I'm not much of a cook, and anyway they're more than good, they're great!

I threw on some purple and black Hollister yoga pants and a lace tank top. I drove quickly to the Chocolate Shoppe and bought some chocolate covered toffee, her favorite. Of course they're my favorite too so I had to get myself a little. There was a giant Get Well Soon balloon; it was four times the size of a normal balloon. I just had to get it for Joc.

*

Flashback

I walked into my sister's room and she looked like crap. She didn't seem any better since the last time I saw her. She was still all bandaged up and still in an ugly hospital gown. Can't they make them a better color than puke green? Mom was sleeping in the uncomfortable matching puke green hospital chair.

"Hey Jocelyn, how are you feeling?" I said trying not to make my eyes droop with sadness as I looked down at the glum white hospital floor.

"Oh hey sis, I'm doing a lot better. They have controlled the bleeding, but my liver is bruised so I have to see another specialist. Hopefully, I can still go home on Sunday," she said looking hopeful.

I didn't even want to tell her we were planning a party. She loves planning parties.

"I am sorry this happened to you." Since it's all my fault.

"Me too. And now I'm starting to think someone did this on purpose."

She shut the drape around us, as if that was going to keep people from hearing our conversation.

"What? What do you mean?" I was trying to cover up the fact that I was shaking and nervous. What am I supposed to tell her? That she is hurt because of me. There is a killer on the loose that wants to destroy my whole family.

"Someone sent me a text that said, *sorry you didn't die, but next time you will.* Who do you think would send that? Do you think it is a joke or does someone really want to hurt me?" She didn't seem fazed by the message. That's because she doesn't know the truth.

"Oh my God Jocelyn. You didn't tell mom or the police anything did you?"

"Of course not, mom would freak out."

"Okay, well I will try to figure this out for you. I'll call the cell phone company to see if they can trace the text." But of course I knew it was from my killer. I wish I could trace the text back to a phone but I was sure it was sent from a throw away prepaid phone just like the ones I was sent.

"Thanks sis. I am sure it's nothing. But I don't know. I got a couple of weird texts before the accident. That's what I wanted to tell you the other night when I came in your room, but it looked like you were pissed so I didn't bother. So, what's in the box?" She asked changing the subject.

Wait, she's been getting texts longer than me?

"Oh yeah, I almost forgot to give it to you. It's your favorite," I said slipping it onto the bed. She opened the foil wrap, "Cool. Chocolate covered toffee. Thanks!" She said with a huge smile from ear to ear.

Flashback

"Do you think we should wake mom up?" I asked.

"Nah let her sleep. I think this is the first time she has actually slept since I got here. She's been a nervous wreck."

"I'm sure, she loves you so much. And she just lost dad. If she lost one of us too, she would be ruined."

If she only knew how much danger we were in. That she might lose me sooner than she thinks. I need to find my killer before he finds me. I can't put my mom through that again.

"I think one of the specialists is coming in soon. You can get going Isabelle, you don't have to stay to hear what he has to say."

"Okay, if you don't mind. I'll get going. I have a lot of work to make up for school. I love you; let me know if you need anything!" I gave her a hug and a kiss and said goodbye.

I left the hospital more scared than ever. This jerk has gotten to my sister and is threatening her too. I didn't want to be alone tonight. I wished my mom was coming home. I wished Erik wasn't mad at me. I didn't want Chris or James to think I was afraid because I needed some space. So, I didn't bother texting either of them.

When I got home I set the alarm and made sure all the windows and doors were locked. Not like that would stop a powerful vampire, but it made me feel better. I ate the leftover Chinese food and put the movie Grown-Ups on. I needed to laugh even if it was alone. I fell asleep in my dad's recliner watching the movie.

*

"Hey man you got a beer?"

"Holy crap, you look familiar."

"Dude, so do you."

At the same time they said each other's names. James – Chris. They were sitting next to a huge fire that looked to be in the middle of nowhere. James handed him the beer.

"Chris, how many years has it been?"

"Dude like ninety. I haven't seen you since Katherine died. What have you been up to all these years?"

"Well my biggest accomplishment is that I invented the airplane with Wilbur and Orville Wright in 1903. We were best buds back then, they basically stole my idea," said James.

"Man, that's rough."

"I know, can we drop the act and stop talking like damn hippies?"

Flashback

"Oh thank God," Chris said laughing. He put his hands over the fire to warm them up.

"What about you? What have you been up to?" James asked.

"Same old crap. I bought a ranch in Colorado with my wife in the forties. She knew I was a vampire. They were the best years of my life. We were married for four years before she was killed by I think, werewolves." He spat. "I tried to track them for years but never could figure it out. I lived a long time there alone and then I made my way to Nevada," Chris explained.

"Wow. So, why are you hanging out with a bunch of hippies?"

"Well, I heard they were getting some people together to protest the Vietnam War. Once we get enough people they are heading to Washington," Chris said taking a sip of his beer.

"That's exactly why I'm here too. You know I think war is no good. All the stuff I saw, I wouldn't want anyone to witness."

"I know, if we could get all the vampires in the world together we could stop the war."

"Nice thought, but you know half of us aren't good," James laughed. "You got a car? Or are you taking one of the buses."

"I've got a nice new green VW Beetle. You should check it out. And if we end up going to Washington you can hitch a ride with me."

"Okay, bro, that sounds great."

Chapter 27: I just want a Good Night's Sleep

Oh my God. What was that crazy dream? Chris and James have been friends all this time? And what the heck was Chris wearing? I am going to have to bust his chops about those red bellbottoms and stupid headband. And, what's with James' beard? It looked like he hadn't shaved in 3 years.

I was so confused about the dream I just had. I looked at the television and it was 2 am. I went into my parent's room to sleep. I hadn't gone in there since my dad died. I went in his closet and took out a soft grey Nautica sweatshirt. I wrapped myself up in it. I also took his favorite blue fleece blanket out. I laid in their bed and covered myself up. I scanned the pictures of our family that hung on the walls. I cried myself to sleep as I stared at a photo of my father and me riding bikes together.　　*

"Isabelle, honey, look what daddy got you for your 6th birthday."

"A Barbie bike! Daddy, I love it so much." I wrapped my arms around my dad so tight. It was a bright pink bike with purple letters that said Barbie on it. It had a white basket and a bell. Glittery purple tinsel hung off the handlebars.

"There's no training wheels Iz, so now you have to learn how to ride without them."

"I don't know if I can do it, can't you put the wheels on it daddy?"

He laughed, "Sweetie, I will spend all day today teaching you if that's what it takes, now put your helmet on." He handed me a matching pink helmet that said my name across the back in purple glitter.

My dad and I spent hours going up and down our street. He held my bike at the sides and let me go just long enough to peddle a couple of times. By the afternoon, I was riding my bike up and down the street all by myself.

"I am so proud of you Isabelle. Let's go get some ice-cream."

Chapter 28: So Much to Do

I woke up in my parent's bed. I had just had a wonderful flashback about my childhood. I had the best day with my dad on my 6th birthday. When I was little all my birthdays were fun. As I got older I began to hate my birthdays. But it was always nice to remember the good times I had with my dad. I miss him so much, that even my wonderful memories won't stop the pain.

I had to get myself together so I could concentrate on all the work I had to make up for school. It's better to get it done sooner than later. I really was not looking forward to writing a paper on Charles Dickens.

The doorbell rang.

"Knock, knock, it's James." I could hear James through the door, so I knew it was okay to open it.

"Hey James, whatcha doin' here?" I asked, opening

the door.

"Came to check on my little sis. What else would I be doing here?"

"Thanks, I could actually use the company. I had a rough night." I said leading him into the kitchen.

You look like you just woke up," He laughed.

"I did," I giggled back. "I haven't even eaten yet, have you?"

"Um, well no, because I don't eat, remember."

"Oh yeah, sorry."

"Hey, let me whip you up something. I haven't cooked in a while."

I sat down at the kitchen table while he searched through the cabinets for a mixing bowl and spatula. I had a million questions for him. I didn't know where to begin. I wanted to ask him about the vision I had of him and Chris in the late sixties. But I didn't want to freak him out. Can you freak a vampire out? I laughed to myself.

"So, have you and Chris been friends all these years?" I finally asked.

"We lost touch after you passed and I went to war. I didn't see him for years. I met up with him about forty years ago. It was the weirdest thing." He whisked the mix quickly.

"Wow, that is amazing. I can't believe you remained

friends for so long." I took a large gulp of my coffee. I was starving and couldn't wait to eat.

"Yeah well when you finally own a telephone it is pretty easy," he laughed.

"I guess so," I laughed back. "So, how did you guys meet in the sixties?" I really needed to confirm my vision.

"I met him at a bonfire in Nevada where people were gathering to protest against the war, the Vietnam War," he laughed, "I forget how many wars I have lived through sometimes."

"Oh my God, what were you wearing?"

"Wha--att?" James was hysterically laughing now.

"How the hell am I supposed to know what I was wearing forty years ago, are you crazy?" He almost dropped the mix all over the counter instead of on the hot griddle.

"No, but I think I am going crazy! I had a dream about you guys, when you met, it was at a bonfire. Now, I am dreaming about a past I wasn't even in. My life is so perplexing!" I was freaking out now.

"Isabelle, calm down. You will figure your whole life out soon. It's complicated. Our whole world is complicated."

"You vampires don't like to help me. I'll figure my life out on my own I guess." I rolled my eyes and turned my head away.

"Isabelle, look at me, we are all here to help and protect you. We first need to eliminate your killer then we can figure our life out. Chris and Erik know things that I can't explain. So just stop getting yourself all worked up and eat your pancakes." He tossed like 6 pancakes on my plate and sprayed some whip cream all over them.

"Fine. Thank you."

He made the best chocolate chip, banana pancakes I have ever eaten. I wish I remembered how to cook. I know in my old life I was the one who cooked breakfast and dinner for everyone. Now I can't even make eggs, and I used to collect them fresh from the chickens.

"What a difference from back then, huh Isabelle?"

"I know. I was just thinking that. I used to walk out in our backyard and get fresh milk and eggs. Life has changed so much. It must be so strange for you."

"I would say more challenging than anything else. I have learned so much through war, education and technology. I am like a walking history book." He pulled out the kitchen chair and sat down.

"Oh, I almost forgot, I have to write a paper about Charles Dickens. Maybe you can help me." I said giving him my puppy dog eyes.

"Sure, but what are you going to put as a footnote,

James Jackson's brain?" he started laughing.

My iPhone rang. Stewie Griffin said mom, mom,
mama, mama, because that is my ringtone for my mom.
James just looked at me funny. I am not sure he knows what
Family Guy is.

"Hey mom, what's up?" I answered.

"Well, I just wanted to let you know Jocelyn won't be
coming home today. There is now something wrong with her
kidney function. They want to treat her for a couple more
days and hopefully she won't need dialysis."

"Oh no mom, that stinks. I don't think I am going to
make it to the hospital today because I have a lot of work to
catch up on."

"It's alright honey, I think I am just going to come
home later and sleep in my own bed tonight," she said sadly.
"I'll grab us dinner and I'll see you later."

"Kay, bye mom." I hung up and went straight to
working on my paper.

James stayed most of the day and helped me with my
homework. It felt like old times. I loved having him here. He
had to leave before my mom got home so she wouldn't ask
any questions.

Chapter 29: Girl's Night

My mom came home with sushi. My favorite, spicy tuna rolls and sweet potato rolls. Of course she had to get salmon, even though I think it's gross. She kept shoving the salmon rolls in my face with her chopsticks, trying to make me try it.

"Isabelle, you don't know you don't like it if you've never even tried it," she kept saying over and over like a broken record. I think she just didn't really want to talk about anything else.

"So, mom I had a dream about dad. Remember on my 6th birthday, he gave me that Barbie bike." That was the first time I mentioned my dad since he died.

My mom's eyes teared up. "Yeah I remember. You and your dad stayed outside all day going up and down the street. I couldn't believe he taught you to ride it in one day." She said pouring herself a glass of white wine. Then she took

Flashback

a huge swig. My mom never drinks. I think she just needed to take the edge off.

"I know, he was always good at teaching me things. I miss him so much," my eyes began to tear.

My mom reached her hand across the table to touch mine. "I miss him so much too, and I am trying to be strong for your sister."

My text message alert went off and interrupted our conversation. I took my hand away and grabbed my phone.

I am coming for you soon, hope you're ready.

It was from an unknown sender of course. I didn't want my mom to see that I was nervous, so I just looked at the phone and put it back on the table.

"Who's that?" She asked.

"Just Rachael sending me a dumb forward about being best friends," I said trying to cover my butt.

"Well that's nice that she thinks about you and sends you things."

I guess my mom was right. At least I have two friends who love me even though someone else wants to kill me and I am a freak show.

"I know. I'm glad I have such good friends," I smiled.

"Hey do you wanna watch a movie tonight?"

"Sure, honey that sounds good," she said cleaning up. My mom washed all the dishes. She could never leave dishes in the sink no matter what kind of mood she was in.

We watched *Thirteen Going On Thirty*, since that is one of my mom's favorite laugh out loud movies. I got some candy from my secret candy stash and we made popcorn and hot chocolate. We cuddled under the blanket together on the couch. I haven't hung out with my mom like this in years. It felt really good. I wish I could just tell her the truth. I wanted to spill everything in that moment. I know she would love me know matter what, but I am not so sure she would believe me. She probably would have me sent off to some psychiatric ward.

After the movie, I gave her a hug and kiss and went up to bed. Even with everything going on I still had a great night with my mom. I tried not to think about my killer because I wanted a good night's sleep. No flashbacks, no visions, no nothing.

Chapter 30: Dream Anyway

Midnight's hooves struck the dry ground with great force. He wanted to run faster and faster. I made it to town in record time. Christopher was waiting for me at the market. I trotted to the hitching post so I could tie Midnight to it. I was just about to get off the horse when Nathan came towards me.

"Coming to see me, my dear?" He said holding a glass of beer up in the air making it slosh about.

"Not, today Nathan," I sighed dramatically.

"Get off that horse and give me a kiss," he slurred as he put his hand on my ankle and tried to move it up my leg.

Midnight neighed loudly and he removed his hand. I think animals sense evil.

"Nathan, please, I am here to meet a friend," I said

Flashback

trying to get off the horse.

"No wife of mine will be meeting gentlemen in town." His face was in mine and his hot breath stank of alcohol. I don't think I have ever seen him sober. Maybe he will be too drunk to show up for our wedding.

"First of all, I am not your wife; secondly, it is no business of yours who I am meeting."

He grabbed my arm firmly, "Listen here, you will do as I say, for you are to be my wife."

I took my other hand and pushed his hand off of me.

Just then Christopher came over to us. "Is there a problem here Nathan?" He asked sharply.

"I am having a conversation with my fiancée, and it does not concern you."

"It does concern me when I see a man putting his hands on a woman, so I suggest you don't ever do that again." Christopher's eyes looked fierce. I had never seen him so angry before.

"And, what are you to do about it, peasant?" Nathan, spat on Christopher's boot.

Christopher grabbed the stein out of Nathan's hand and threw it to the ground. He then took Nathan's left arm and twisted it behind his back. He pushed Nathan into the dirt. "That's what I am going to do about it you pompous jerk.

Now be on your way and leave the lady be."

Nathan dragged himself off the ground and stumbled down the road towards his house.

*

Wow. I woke up Monday morning the sun was so bright shining through my black curtains. It made me squint as I tried to open my tired eyes. I thought about what a great friend Chris was. I don't know how Erik could ever have thought that he is my killer. He protected me just as much as Erik did but I never realized it. I grabbed my iphone off the table next to my bed. There was another text message from the unknown sender.

Isabelle, I can't wait to see you again.

I knew it was from my killer. It was from a blocked number as usual. It wasn't from someone who wanted to see me for a good reason. I was getting sick of all the messages that led nowhere. I needed to come up with a plan, a way to catch my killer. I didn't want to go to school, I just wanted to stay home and think about what to do.

I got out of bed and went down the hall to my parent's room. The bedroom door was open and my mom was still lying in bed. I went over to the bed and got under the soft tan comforter on my dad's side.

"Hey, mom, I didn't get a lot of sleep last night, can I stay home from school today?"

My mom stroked my hair and put her face close to mine on the pillow. "Of course you can honey, we've had a long week."

"Thanks, mom. I don't think I am going to come to the hospital with you either."

"That's okay; I will go around lunch time and bring Jocelyn something to eat."

I spent the day writing down all the things that had happened to me and what my killer had told me. I sat on my bedroom floor and started with a time line of when my anonymous phone calls began. The second thing I wrote down was the day I had the dream of my father's text. I couldn't figure out why my father was texting Evelyn. Then my sister said her texts began a week before the accident. I was frustrated and I couldn't put all the pieces together.

"Uh," I yelled loudly as I threw all my notes in the air. I really needed to talk to Jocelyn again, but that would have to wait. I was too hungry to think anymore so I ordered take out from the Sand Crab Café. After I ate dinner, I lay in bed watching reruns of Friends until I faded off to sleep.

Chapter 31: Yet Another Flashback

I tossed and turned in my bed. I couldn't wake myself up from the nightmare I was in. I was outside in the woods, alone for some reason. The pitch black sky made it hard to see. The moon shined through the bare trees just enough to give light to see my feet. I ran through the woods. I heard branches breaking on the ground, and the sound of rustling leaves being blown by the wind. A blue light gleamed from farther into the forest. I quickly tensed up when I heard footsteps behind me. It could be an animal, I thought. Although, animals don't make that much noise, except for bears, or maybe a mountain lion. But there are no mountain lions in Connecticut. It has to be a person. But why would a person be in the woods in the middle of the night? Then again, I am. I just don't know how I'm here.

I started to run towards the blue light looking for an

escape. I fell over a log from a tree that had fallen down. I hit the ground with a *loud thump.* I had ripped my dress and got dirt all over it. My father was going to kill me if I didn't die here first. I pushed up off the ground, but when I set my foot, pain flared in my ankle. I stood up carefully. Ignoring the pain I started to run as fast as I could to get away. But I couldn't, who or what was too fast. I then surrendered myself.

I was too scared to speak. I saw a shadow of a person coming out of the trees.

"I'm coming for you Katherine," the voice said angrily.

*

I woke up scared out of my wits. It was still dark out, and I couldn't fall back to sleep. Not after the dream I had. It just felt too real. I felt like somebody was trying to get in my head and confuse me. I grabbed my candle, and headed downstairs quietly enough so I wouldn't wake my brothers. I walked out of the door and went outside to see my horses. They always calmed me when I was afraid, especially Midnight. We had a special bond. I stood there for a while stroking my horse. I blew out the candle and plopped down in the hay.

"Katherine, why are you sleeping in here?" Chris asked curiously as he opened the barn door.

Should I tell him about my dream? Well I had to tell somebody.

"I... uhhh," I said groggily but I didn't know how to put it in words.

"Well go on," He urged me as he sat down next to me in the hay.

"I had this dream last night...." I told him the whole thing. "And I think somebody is coming for me," I concluded.

"Wait, hold on. You think somebody is after you? And why would that be?"

"Did I not just tell you my whole entire dream? How could you not think someone is after me after I experienced that?"

"I highly doubt that someone is coming for you. It was just a dream Katherine."

"But how do you explain that it felt so real and it was so vivid?"

"It's not that difficult to explain. You just have an over active imagination that's all," Chris stated.

"You know what Christopher? I think you should go!"

He was making me so angry. I know I'm right. I need to be extra careful now. I'm not stupid.

"What! But I just got here. I thought I could help you with your chores today, and then maybe we could go to town."

"That's right," I said pushing him out of the barn, "Leave. If you don't believe me I don't want you here."

Chapter 32: Not A Normal School Day

I grabbed a waffle out of the freezer, and popped it into the toaster. I waited for my waffle and tried to remember my dreams from the night before. I quickly scrolled through my text messages while I was waiting. There was a new one from Erik. I thought he was still mad at me. I hadn't talked to him in days, since we had gotten into the argument about Chris.

Pick you up for school today? It read.

I responded, *Sure* ☺

See you in 10 he responded back in less than a second.

I nibbled on the waffle a little, but I'm never hungry in the morning, so I threw it out. I guess that was a waste. I heard my doorbell ring and I went to answer. I opened it, and it was Erik.

"You didn't have to come in. You could've just beeped you know." I said even though I was so happy to see him.

I know," He said smiling." Ready to go?"

"Yeah let me just get my bag."

I ran upstairs and shoved some papers in my book bag. I didn't even bother zipping it.

"Okay, I'm ready," I said, my hair all frizzy from running up the stairs. I quickly straightened it out.

"What's this?" Erik asked picking up a paper from the floor.

"Oh that," I said my cheeks reddening with embarrassment, "That's umm a drawing."

"Of what?"

How could he not know it's trees? Maybe he just wants to hear me say it?

"Of trees, with a blue light coming out of it," I said starting to remember what had happened to me in a dream of my old life. I recall being afraid in the woods, running from something. Running towards the blue light.

"Now why would you draw that?" He asked curiously.

"It's just something I've experienced," I said carefully trying to pick the right words so I wouldn't give anything away.

"Okay, you're weird," he said laughing and walking out the door, "You coming?"

"Yeah," I said hurrying after him.

I got in the car and buckled up.

Erik put the stereo on, and put in one of his CDs. The music started playing as he started driving. The song was vaguely familiar. The man began to sing, and I recognized who it was.

"I love this song!" I said as the lead singer of Greenday started singing about an Armageddon flame, and some dogs howling out of key.

We sang to the radio the whole way to school. Erik pretty much butchered all the songs, but it was fun anyway. We pulled in the parking lot with the music pumping.

All of my morning classes were about the same boring things; Charles Dickens and math equations, just to name a few. I couldn't wait for Drama class, or at least lunch. As soon as class was over I rushed to the lunchroom

"Hey," Erik said walking up to me as I strolled to the lunchroom. He put his arm over my shoulder. London gave us dirty looks as she passed us. "Hi," I said smiling.

Hi Iz, hey Erik!" Rachael exclaimed.

"Why hello Erik. Looking fine today," Evelyn said as Erik and I sat down next to each other.

Why does she always have to do that? I shook my head.

"What's wrong?" Erik asked looking under the hair that was surrounding my face.

"Nothing, I...," I started to say when I was cut off.

"Hey Izzy," Chris said sliding in on the other side of me.

Erik gave him a dirty look. So I gave him my 'Be nice' look. Erik ignored it, and kept glaring.

"Well I thought I'd at least try the nickname. But I guess it sucked. I won't call your girlfriend that again," Chris said to Erik emphasizing the girlfriend part. So I guess he noticed all the glaring.

"It's fine Chris," I said sighing. "Right Erik?" I said looking him in the eye. He nodded.

"Well, this is nice and all, but I must get going," Rachael said getting up. "I've got places to go, and people to see."

"Bye," I called after her as she left.

"Hey Iz, Rach and I are going to study for the English test at her house tomorrow if you want to come. I am really over *Charles Dickens* right now."

"Sure I will definitely come. Are you going right after school?"

"Yeah, I'm just gonna go in Rachael's car."

I was going to be late for class, but I had to get my book out of my locker. My bright blue locker wouldn't open. It was stuck. I tried and tried to open it, but it wouldn't budge.

"Can't get it open, loser? Keep trying," I heard a voice say behind me.

"What do you want London?" I asked sighing. Not bothering to turn around.

"Oh sweetie, I'm only trying to help," She said. "Now will you please get out of the way so I can?"

Reluctantly I moved to the side. I needed help. Who cares if it's the devil's spawn? She hit the locker hard with her bony fist, and it opened.

"How did you do that?"

"It's all in the wrist," She said smiling. Obviously she was proud of herself.

Yeah all in the wrist, with her perfect pink manicured daggers. Maybe she's a vampire too?

"Oh," I said lifting my brows.

"Yup, when you have an older brother, you tend to know these things."

"I know what you mean."

She laughed, and not at me for once.

"Why are you being so nice to me?" I asked, "You're always a...." I said before she cut me off.

"A brat to you? So I've heard from Evelyn," she laughed. So, I guess she's heard.

"Yes. But seriously, you're never nice to anyone except for your *posse*," I said with air quotes.

"Like I said at the mall, we're besties forever."

"What?" I was totally taken aback.

"Yes, now if we're going to trick our moms, you have to keep up," She said in her normal 'bratty' voice.

"What? Why?"

"Don't be stupid. My mother wants us to hang out. She thinks I'm coming over your house. Your mom thinks so too."

"Ummm." I was stunned. Why wouldn't my mom tell me? I slammed my locker shut. Just thinking about having to have a conversation with her made my blood curdle. Maybe Erik has some special power he hasn't told me about. It would be nice if he could vanish all thoughts of London from my memory.

"Well, I'll see you after school. I assume you want me to drive you, yes?"

I nodded. I didn't know what I was supposed to do. I don't want to hang out with *her*.

She walked away, and I started walking to class. If I hurried, I could make it to class before the bell rang. I ran down the hallway and up the stairs. I was out of breath. I ran in the classroom as soon as the teacher was about to close the door. I almost bumped into her on my way in. Luckily she didn't call me out or write me up.

A bunch of kids snickered at me. I didn't even bother acknowledging them.

I walked to my computer and started working. Someone threw a piece of paper at me. I opened it expecting it was a note.

What was that all about? Bumping into the teacher, and almost being late. You're never late. Please don't tell me that you were kissing Erik. Oh God. I don't even want to think about that. Well anyways, did Ev ask you if you wanted to come over tomorrow? We'll study for the big test on Friday. Ugh, I hate reading. Especially when reading Charles Dickens. Why can't we read the Lying Game? I love that show, I really wanna read the book. It would be the perfect book to read. It wouldn't bore me to death, and I actually wouldn't fall asleep in class for once.

-Rachael

I wrote back to her.

Flashback

London is what happened. I couldn't open my locker, and she just showed up. She was being all nice up until she told me that she's coming over today. Apparently her mother and mine think we're friends, and that we're going to hang out today. She's even bringing me home! I really can't believe I have to hang out with her. Oh and BTW, yes Ev told me. I'm coming, and I'll pick up Dunkin' Donuts on the way.

Iz

I threw the note to her when the teacher wasn't looking. She was busy talking to another teacher like all teachers do. Rachael quickly read it, and replied.

OMG! I would totally die! I can't stand her. I could never be in an enclosed room with her without fighting the urge to claw her eyes out. She has a lot of nerve to make up such bs. You guys are totally the best of friends! Just like I'm still best friends with Rikki! I mean come on. Still, it's gonna be fine. You'll live. & okay, see you at my house tomorrow then? I didn't bother responding. I just nodded to her and got back to working on my project.

*

I wasn't really paying attention in my next class. It was all just a blur to me. I zoned out a couple of times, but my phone vibrated in my book bag, so it brought me back. I stuck my hand in my bag and looked at it quickly.

Four more days until your birthday.
Well, that is if you make it that far.

I shivered and looked around the room. I felt like somebody was watching me. I rushed out of the classroom and went to Drama. I just wanted to get away from all of this. My life is a complete mess.

When I got in the classroom I sat right down, and put my hands over my face. "Hey," I heard Erik say as he sat down next to me.

"Hi," I mumbled through my hands.

"Are you okay?" He asked concerned.

"Yeah, I'm fine see," I said taking my hands off of my face and smiling. "

"Do you want to talk about it?"

I didn't say anything, I just handed him my phone. He scrolled through all of the text messages that I had gotten from the unknown sender.

"Him again? Iz, I told you, you don't have to worry, I'll protect you."

"You mean we'll protect her," Chris said sitting next to Erik and putting his arm around him like they were best buds. Erik obviously didn't like him, and flinched away from.

"Umm okay, guys, I really don't want to deal with this in school, so if you don't mind." I said turning towards the teacher as she entered the room.

Alright class, as we all know, we will be practicing for the play today. Christopher," she said using his full name, "Come up to the front of the class."

Groaning, he went up.

"Now class, I have made Chris one of the leads in the play. You may go check the bulletin board to see your part. I have now cast every one of them."

Everybody got up to read the casting. I didn't need to look to know what part I would be playing, but I went up anyway. The paper read:

Castings:

Hermia- Isabelle Halloway

Lysander- Aidan Parker

Puck- Christopher Smython

Oberon- Liam Wilson

Helena- Adriana Harris

The list went on and on, but I only focused on one part.

Tree- Erik Landon

I couldn't believe it. I know Erik's bad, but not that bad. At least he'll make a hot tree.

Chris started laughing, but I didn't. I thought he was being stupid.

"I'm only doing this for you. If you didn't care about him, I would've already ripped his head off," Erik said in my mind.

Erik!" I replied.

"Well it's true," He said back shrugging.

I ignored him and got in my spot for rehearsal.

We spent 45 minutes practicing for the play. Ugh, that was tiring. I just wanted to go home and relax.

I really didn't want to deal with London, but I walked outside anyway. She was waiting for me next to her blue Porsche. She texted on her be-dazzled iPhone while she tapped her four inch pink Louis Vuitton heels on the asphalt.

Reluctantly, I walked over to her.

"Hi," she said as she got in the car. "Took you long enough, I've been waiting for like five minutes."

Wow, five minutes, that's a really big deal. London never has to wait for a thing in her life.

I got in the car and didn't respond. Her car was really

nice. It had leather seats, and all the bells and whistles. It was just perfect. It made my Mercedes look like a garbage truck.

When we got to my house my mom was home from the hospital, she baked cookies and had glasses of milk on the kitchen table. How embarrassing, does she think I am ten?

"Thanks, Mrs. Halloway, that was so nice of you," London said in her fake, sweet voice to my mother. I am sure she is going to text everybody in school what a loser I am. I really didn't want to spend my day acting like London was my best friend.

"You're welcome sweetie," My mom said. "Well, I'll leave you two alone. I've got to head to the store anyway. Do you need anything honey?" My mom asked me.

"No mother," I said sighing. I really wanted to tell her to bring me home some big B repellent.

"Okay, well then I've got to get going," she said grabbing her purse and heading out the door.

"Well," London said leaning on my counter, "What do you want to do, now that I'm stuck here in this dreadful place?" She asked looking around my house like it was a homeless shelter.

"Believe me," I sighed, "I'm not that ecstatic either. But just suck it up and deal with it."

"Well then, I will. Oooohhh! I want to see your room!
I bet that it's going to be a hot mess. At least your clothes are
cute," she said looking me up and down.

"I wish I could say the same about your face," I
laughed. "Just kidding." Or am I?

"Whatever, let's just go see your room."

We headed up to my room. She stood there
observing my blue walls with black flowers and vines. Then
she moved on to my bed with fluffy purple pillows, a blue
comforter, and my pretty metallic stand up light that had fake
crystals hanging down it. Next, she looked at my small flat
screen TV on top of my dresser. Finally, her eyes moved to my
guitar, standing up in the corner of my room.

"Wow, your room's actually pretty. Well what are the
odds? Now I don't have anything embarrassing about you to
tell the whole school. I really underestimated you." She said
shocked.

"I guess you did," I said shrugging.

"Got anything good to watch?" She said plopping
down on my bed.

"I've got *Silence of the Lambs*, if you're not too scared
to watch it," I giggled.

"I love that movie!" She exclaimed.

Really? London Carter and I liked the same thing? I was surprised. I took the DVD out of the case and threw it in the player.

"I'll be right back, I'm going to make some popcorn." I went down stairs and left her in my room, hoping she wouldn't go through my stuff. If she found my I heart Vampires stickers I would never hear the end of it from her or everyone at school.

When I came back up she was just chilling on my bed looking through Teen magazine.

"Let's watch the movie, already." London said sarcastically, back to her old self again.

We sat on my bed anxiously watching the movie and repeated all of our favorite lines, which all happened to be the same. I was really enjoying myself. I'm just not sure she really was.

When the movie ended she hugged me good bye. "Thanks for having me over Iz, I had a really good time."

"Me too," I said sincerely. I couldn't wait to hear the rumors about me when I got to school the next day.

Chapter 33: Another Ridiculous Flashback

"**What** happened to you the other day at the market? Chris told me that something had happened with you and Nathan, but he didn't really explain what," Lillian asked while putting the finishing touches on the dress she was making.

"Nathan was just being Nathan as usual. You know how he is," I said staring at the dress she was making. It was a beautiful purple dress with white lace on it.

"Oh Katherine, was he intoxicated again? How are you going to have children with that man let alone live with him?" She asked putting the needle and thread down. She picked up the dress and held it in front of me.

"I honestly don't know." I said shaking my head.

Flashback

Ignoring me she said, "This will look absolutely beautiful on you!"

"What?" I asked taken aback, "I thought this was for your mother."

"No silly, it's for you. Think of it as an I'm so sorry you have to marry such scum present." She said handing it to me.

"Thank you; I don't know what to say."

"You don't have to say anything. Just wear it."

"Oh, I definitely will." I ran my fingers up and down the lace bottom. Lillian is such a talented dress maker. My clothes usually come out crooked.

"Good. So, what did Erik say when you told him?"

"Told him what?"

She stood there gawking at me. "We were just talking about it! How do you not remember a conversation that we had less than two minutes ago?"

"Oh sorry," I said stupidly.

"Well what did you tell him?"

"I didn't tell him anything. I haven't seen him in two days."

"Then what are you going to tell him when you see him?" She asked. She picked up a blue barrette and folded it back and forth through her bony fingers.

I didn't know what I was going to tell him. I had no clue how he's going to react. I didn't want to relive what happened at the ball.

"The same thing I told you."

"That wasn't a lot of information. If you love him you shouldn't keep anything from him. I wouldn't, if Chris loved me back," Lily said sadly.

She grabbed my shoulders and spun me around so that my back was to her. She began to play with my hair and put the barrette in it.

"Oh Lily, I'm sorry. If there's any way I can help you I will do it. Maybe we can think of a way to get Chris to court you.

"That might be a great idea," Lillian said nodding like she had a plan. "Your hair looks beautiful up like this.

I walked toward the mirror and held my hair up with my hand right hand. I moved my gold necklace up and down my neck with my other hand.

Lillian stood behind me in the mirror. "You are so lucky that Erik wants to be with you."

I stared at her eyes in her reflection. "You are just as lucky as I Lillian, you and Chris will be together soon."

Chapter 34: Rachael's

I was groggy, but my mind raced with thoughts. I wondered if Lillian and Chris ever got together. Maybe I will ask him about her later. I tried not to think about the fact that it's my birthday in three days. I'm scared but yet anxious about who my killer is, and what he'll do to me. I didn't want to get ready for school, but I had to. I missed too many days already.

I had the worst migraine at school all day. I honestly don't even remember half my day. My head hurt so bad, that I couldn't even really practice for the play. Ms. Gale was so nice to me; she let me watch everyone else. Erik and Chris were both doting on me, and fighting over who should get me a bottle of water. I am so over them right now.

I really didn't feel like going to Rachael's to study. I felt dizzy, like I was going to pass out. I probably shouldn't even have been driving. I drove slowly to Dunkin' Donuts. I ordered a couple of coffees and some chocolate chip muffins. By the time I got there, Evelyn and Rachael were already studying.

"What took you so long, Iz? We're having caffeine withdrawal," Rachael said when I walked in. Like Rachael needs any more caffeine, she's hyper enough.

Rachael only lives a couple of blocks from me, but she lives right on the beach. Her house is a grey, oversized Cape Cod. It has an awesome white deck that comes off the back and you can walk right onto the beach. Sometimes after a storm the waves are so high; they come right up to the top of the deck. We usually hang out at her house on our days off. We rarely go to Evelyn's because her mom is a neat freak and we can't make a mess.

"Here's your mocha coffee with nine sugars and skim milk," I said rolling my eyes.

"You're funny, ha, ha," Rachael said grabbing the coffee cup eagerly.

"Thanks Isabelle, this will definitely help us get through Charles Dickens," Evelyn said sighing.

I've got a bad headache today but I guess I'm ready to study. So, what have you girls studied so far?" I asked as I sat down on Rachael's leopard couch.

The inside of Rachael's house looked like Lady Gaga's closet had thrown up all over it. Every room had a different pattern from zebra to polka dots. Don't get me wrong her house is beautiful, there's just a whole lot going on in one little place.

"I've got aspirin in my bag if you want some," Evelyn said.

"I'm good; I just took one, thanks."

"We were just talking about the symbolism of the names in the book. We know that is going to be on the test," Rachael said.

"Oh, that's easy, Oliver's name is Twist because of all the reversals of fortune that he experiences," I explained. I continued to talk about the symbolism of Bulls-eye and then I realized they were just staring at me. I think I went too far.

Rachael looked at me in disbelief. "What the hell are you talking about?" She said.

Evelyn glared at me like she knew something, "Um, I didn't know you were so into this book, I thought we both agreed that Pretty Little Liars should be the book we read for English Lit."

"Hey, I thought we said The Lying Game," Rachael exclaimed.

"Okay, we are getting off the subject," I said laughing.

"We are never gonna get through this, you two. I read a lot online last night that might help us."

"Okay, we'll be serious," Evelyn said.

We spent three hours studying, well, mostly me telling them everything about the book the author, and them taking notes. We better all get As after I endured the boringness of teaching Charles Dickens.

I realized it was time for dinner and my mom was eating home tonight.

When I got home my mom had dinner on the table. I guess she felt up to cooking again because she had made stuffed shells and garlic bread.

"Mom, how was Jocelyn feeling today?" I asked worried.

"Well, she has to have a couple more tests early tomorrow but she's in great spirits, considering everything that is going on, and she wants you to call her."

"I know mom, Erik and I are going to go visit her tomorrow."

I went straight to my room after dinner. I opened my bedroom door, and I saw someone in it, his back to me. He had on all black with a hoodie over his head. I ran to my sister's room across the hall, and got her baseball bat. The person's back was still facing me, so I snuck up on him and swung the bat. He turned around fast, and caught it in his hand. I screamed!

"Chill Iz, it's just me," said Erik.

"Oh thank God," I said sighing with relief.

"Who'd you think it was?" He asked laughing. He handed me the bat, and went to turn the light on.

"That was not funny. You scared the crap out of me." I said scolding him.

He still had a huge smirk on his face.

"And will you take the damn hoodie off," I said smacking his arm as hard as I could. Of course he probably didn't feel a thing.

"Fine," he said taking it off.

"Why are you here?" I asked.

"Do I need a reason to see you? Not to mention someone's after you." He said solemnly.

"I guess. Oh, you should come to the hospital with me tomorrow. Maybe we can ask Jocelyn some questions about what happened to her?" I asked hopefully.

Maybe he can get things out of her that I can't. He can read her thoughts, I can't.

"Yeah, I'll go. You want me to pick you up for school tomorrow?"

"Sure, but you better go before my mom comes

upstairs. She's pretty exhausted from staying with Joc all day. Plus, she has to get up early to go to the hospital tomorrow; Jocelyn has to have more tests."

He kissed me quickly on the cheek, and went out of my window.

I felt the touch of his lips linger on my cheek. I am sure I will have some good dreams tonight.

Chapter 35: Lillian

"I'm not sure this is a good idea," Lillian said sounding sick to her stomach as we walked to town.

"It was your idea Lil! You're going to have to deal with it if you ever want to be with Chris!" I said exasperatedly.

I could tell Lillian was nervous, but we have been planning this for two days. She seemed so confident about it before, and now she's getting cold feet?

"No, it wasn't. It was originally your idea. I wouldn't have agreed to this if you didn't talk me into it." Lillian said in her defense.

"Well we both know I'm the rebellious one." I laughed. "Still, I don't care if you're nervous. We are going through with the plan just like we said. You'll bring him lunch like we planned, and then you'll trip and he'll catch you. It's

Flashback

not that original, but that's all we've got."

"Fine," she said sighing. She picked up her skirt as we walked over to Chris's house.

"Why are you doing that? I told you to flirt, not pick up your dress like a floozy!"

"Sorry," She muttered putting her skirt down.

"Chris will think you look beautiful with your new dress on!" I exclaimed.

The previous day we had gone to the market to buy Lillian things to make Chris notice her more. We got her a dress, shoes, hair accessories, and got her hair done.

"You think?" She asked blushing.

"Yes." I stated. "Now let's go. He's right there." I said pointing to him on the hill.

We walked up the hill to Chris, and Lillian handed him the basket of food.

"Thank you," he said taking it.

"Well don't just stand there! Go eat." I pushed her towards him.

"Aren't you coming Katherine?" Lillian asked.

"No, I have to go meet Erik. I'll catch up with you guys later." I said walking down the hill.

When they weren't looking, I snuck back up and hid behind a tree.

"Sooooo…" Lillian said.

"Well, I suppose we should sit down and enjoy our lunch." Chris pointed to the basket as if Lillian should know to take the blanket out and find a place to lay it on the ground.

They walked to a flat part of the hill, and Lillian pretended to fall. Chris caught her, and they stayed in that position for a while, just staring into each other's eyes. Finally, Lillian broke their gaze and said, "Let me get everything out of the basket so we can eat."

Lillian laid out the picnic beautifully, yet they seemed to be uncomfortable around each other. They started laughing about something, and the awkwardness suddenly stopped. They looked like they were having a great time, so I left them wondering what would happen after their romantic rendezvous.

Chapter 36: 2 Days until My Birthday

School is so redundant. Every day is the same old boring things and it was hard for me to focus with everything else going on. I felt nervous all the time, like someone was constantly watching my every move. I kept thinking about Lillian and Chris too. They must have ended up together. How great for Chris!

Practicing for the play is the only reason I like to go to school lately, but I just really needed the school day to be over. I hadn't had time to go see Jocelyn in the hospital and rack her brain.

Erik and I headed to the hospital right after school. We grabbed some coffee and French crullers to bring to my sister. I should really own a Dunkin' Donuts chain; my friends and I would be eighty percent of the business.

I walked in the room and the doctor was talking to Jocelyn and my mom. He said she needed to stay a couple more days, until her infection was completely gone. I didn't want to tell her we were having a party for my birthday. She loves parties and dancing and she was going to have to miss it.

"Hey," Jocelyn said looking at Erik. "Thanks for visiting me. I see you and my sister made up," she said looking at our intertwined hands.

"Yeah, Joc." I said annoyed and turned to my mom. "Hey mom?" I asked.

"Yes?" She asked looking away from the doctor.

"Can we umm, talk to Joc alone for a minute?"

"Sure, the doctor and I have some matters we have to discuss in private." She said walking out the door with him, but left it open.

Erik went and shut it.

"Okay, what's this all about?" Jocelyn asked.

"Have you gotten anymore texts?" I asked.

"No, I haven't." Her eyes narrowed.

Erik looked at her curiously. "She's lying, don't listen to her. She got a text today. It said, *If you tell anyone what really happened, I'll kill you. You won't get a second chance.*" Erik said.

"No Iz, he's lying. You shouldn't trust him, trust me. Besides, how would he know if I was lying? What is he, a freakin' mind reader?" She laughed crazily.

"No, I read your texts when you weren't paying attention," he said covering it up.

"YOU DID WHAT!!!" She screamed.

"Well someone has to protect you. Your sister told me that she thought someone was after you."

"Why would you say that Iz? I thought we agreed to tell no one," she said looking hurt.

"No, we agreed not to tell mom. You didn't say anything about not telling my boyfriend."

"Oh now he's your boyfriend?" She said sarcastically.

"Yeah he is. Stop trying to change the subject. We need to figure out who is texting you and why. Erik can help us."

"Why are you so interested in who is texting me? It's probably just some ex-boyfriend being a jerk."

"You need to take this seriously, Jocelyn, it's not a joke," Erik said. He looked serious. He was not to be taken lightly.

"You guys are creeping me out! What is the big deal?"

"There maybe someone after us, Joc. We need to protect you," I said leaning closer to her hospital bed.

"Why would anyone be after us?" That makes no sense," Jocelyn exclaimed.

"Um, we are trying to figure that out, I can't get into all the details right now. But we really need to know what you think you saw when you got into the accident."

"Iz, this seems a little crazy, but it really looked like a man. He seemed to be moving with super speed. But after I swerved not to hit him and crashed, I thought I saw him standing over me before I passed out."

"What did he have on?" Erik asked.

"Just looked like black clothes, but he definitely had a hood on, and I couldn't make out his face. Do you think you know him?"

Doesn't this guy have any other clothes besides a hoodie and black pants? I had to think of something quick as to why someone would be after a couple of teenage girls.

"I...I think dad was in trouble and now we are too." I said rubbing her leg through the rough ugly hospital blanket.

"What! What could dad have possibly done to get him in trouble? He was like the most honest man ever."

She looked like she was about to cry. Jocelyn admired our dad so much. I am sure the thought of him doing something wrong tore her up inside.

"That's what we are trying to figure out. Have you

gotten any phone calls or suspicious things while you have been here?"

"I got some cookie bloomers yesterday. I didn't even open them yet and there wasn't even a card! Do you think that is weird?" Jocelyn said.

Erik quickly got up and inspected the cookies. There didn't seem to be anything wrong with them but he threw them out anyway.

"Why would you do that? I wanted to eat them when I feel better!" Jocelyn yelled at him.

"We can't take any chances," I said trying to calm her down.

Just then my mom came back in the room.

"How's everyone doing? Jocelyn, your infection has not spread and the doctor is optimistic that you will be home on Sunday," my mom explained.

"Great. So, I don't get to celebrate Isabelle's birthday," she said disappointed.

"Don't worry, I will order a cake and we can celebrate on Sunday," my mom said with sad eyes looking right at me. "And I'm coming home to sleep tonight, probably late though."

"We need to get going Iz," Erik whispered to me.

"Jocelyn, we are going to head home now. We will

totally celebrate on Sunday. I will call Gram and Papa and tell them to come too. I love you and will call you later," I said getting up and giving her a big hug.

I hugged my mom and then Erik hugged them both too. It was so sweet. I wish I could just explain everything to them so this nightmare could be over.

Erik and I went to Koko Beach for dinner. It is one of my favorite restaurants in Carlsbad. It is close to my house, right on the Boulevard.

I was starving, of course he was not. I got fried calamari strips and he ordered a Chicken Caesar salad. He pretended to eat it every time our waitress came over, but I really ate the whole thing.

My phone rang while we were eating. It was from an anonymous number. Erik saw it and swiftly grabbed it.

"Hello," he said answering my phone.

No one spoke, there was just heaving breathing.

"Answer me you coward!" He yelled. Everyone at the restaurant turned and looked at him. He looked really mad. I haven't seen him this angry since the night of the ball.

"Calm down, we are at a restaurant." I gestured my hand towards him.

"I will come find you, you will not get to my girlfriend," he screamed again and slammed down the phone.

Yeah, break my $300 iPhone that I bought after I had to endure last summer working at Dunkin' Donuts with a crazy stalker guy.

People were really staring at us now. I waved the waitress over. "We really need the bill," I said.

She looked at Erik like he was crazy and nervously put the bill on the table.

I opened the black holder and threw some cash in it and we left. The waitress must have gotten a big tip because I didn't even really count it.

Chapter 37: Friday

Oh my God who is calling me at 5:00 A.M.? I picked up even though it was an anonymous call.

"Hello?" I asked tiredly.

There was no answer, just a bunch of breathing.

"Okay, seriously? It's five o'clock in the freakin' morning. I don't want to deal with this crap, so just answer me."

The person continued to breathe heavily without saying a word. I was annoyed and slammed the phone down. I rolled over and went back to sleep.

"It's Friday" blared in my ears. Seriously, I had to wake up to that song? I felt like I only slept for five minutes. Now it's seven, and I'm gonna be late for school. I quickly put on my skinny jeans, and my purple lace tank top. I ran down

Flashback

the stairs shoving everything in my bag. I didn't even say goodbye to my mother.

*

I arrived in school, and I was the only one in the parking lot. Everyone was already in class. I didn't even have a chance to go to my locker. I missed homeroom again, and went straight to first period.

As usual I couldn't wait to go home. The only thing I looked forward to was watching Erik be a tree. It's hysterical; he wobbles around the stage when we practice. He's such a dork sometimes, but he looks hot in everything he wears.

I was the first one to get to drama club. I started rehearsing my lines, when my phone rang. I clenched my teeth. I didn't need caller ID to know who it was. I answered the phone.

"Hello? What do you want?"

"I just want to know what you want for your birthday."

I was surprised he finally spoke. He usually sits on the phone breathing like a smoker with emphysema. I started shaking, and yelled. "I want you to go to hell!"

Erik came in and said, "What is going on?"

I shushed him.

"Oh honey, I'm already damned, and as we all know, your boyfriend is too. You should give him one message for me. Stay the hell out of my way." And with that, he hung up.

I trembled.

My eyes filled up with tears. Just then Ms. Gale walked in.

"What's wrong?" She said putting her hand on my head. "My sister is not going to be home from the hospital for my birthday tomorrow." I lied. Ugh, I hate lying. My whole life is one big giant lie. "I'm fine, I'm okay now."

"Okay, just let me know if you need anything." She walked away.

I sat in my usual spot on the stage, next to Erik, and she started class. We rehearsed an extra two hours after school, so I didn't have any time to talk to Erik about the phone call.

When we finally got out of school I was starving and totally craving an egg and cheese. I asked Erik to come with me to 101 Café in Oceanside since they serve breakfast all day long. I always feel bad about eating around him, but I didn't want to sit there alone. He had his own car so he followed me.

As I drove down Highway 101 a grey Suburban came into my lane on the other side. It almost ran me off the road. I ended up swerving to avoid him and pulled over on the shoulder. Erik stopped behind me and got out of his car. I was shaking and didn't want to drive.

"Do you think that was on purpose?" I quivered.

"I don't know Iz, but we need to be careful. He hugged me tightly. "The diner is right down the street. Just drive there and we can leave your car at the café if you want."

I agreed and continued to the diner.

We pulled up to the diner and there was a bunch of old-fashioned cars. 101 Café is kind of a local hangout for people who have old cars. I think it's one of the oldest restaurants in Oceanside so people get all nostalgic about it. There are palm trees and old cars painted on the front of the building.

"Hey, I used to have that car except mine was brand new," Erik said laughing and pointing to a red '67 Corvette.

We sat in the checkered booth and I ordered an egg and cheese sandwich and Erik got cheese fries, which of course were for me.

"I don't know what to do anymore Erik," I said nervously. "I'm not going to live in fear anymore. I feel like we didn't get enough information from my sister."

"You're right. We didn't. It's not her fault; she doesn't even know what's going on. James and Chris are trying to contact others to help us track him. I promise he will not get you. If I have to I will wait outside your house all night and protect you."

"What others? Who's going to want to help me?" I said sarcastically.

"There are plenty of vamps out there. When you have lived as long as I have you tend to make a lot of friends that are willing to help."

"I wouldn't know what that's like, I have like two friends." I frowned.

"Isabelle, plenty of people like you, you just choose not to hang out with them."

Yeah, they like me because they don't really know me. If they did they would think I am a freak.

"Whatever, I need to find my killer before I get any new friends."

The waitress came over with our food. I was so hungry I barely stopped eating to talk. I ate my whole sandwich and all the fries.

Erik followed me home because I decided not to leave my car there. My mom was home so he just walked me to the door and didn't come in.

"Hey mom," I said walking in the door. She was in the kitchen washing dishes.

"Hi honey, how was rehearsal?" She asked.

"It was good, I'm just tired. Oh, did I tell you Erik is a tree," I said laughing.

"Oh no, poor Erik," she laughed too.

We couldn't stop giggling about it. It felt good. We hadn't laughed together in awhile.

I gave her a big hug. "I love you mom, I'm going to go shower and read before I go to bed."

"Love you too, Iz," she said.

I laid in bed for a while and read *My Blood Approves* by Amanda Hocking.

I could feel someone outside so I got up and went to my window anxiously. It was just Erik sitting in his car watching my house.

I rested back down on my bed with my feet towards my fluffy black pillows and dialed Erik's number.

"Hello, Iz," he answered.

"What are you doing Erik?" I asked.

"I told you, I will wait outside your house all night

every night to make sure you are okay."

"You really don't have to do that," I said. But I really wanted him to stay. I thought maybe I could get a good night's sleep knowing that he was there, watching over me.

"Get some sleep Iz, I love you."

"Kay. Love you too, bye."

It was easy to fall asleep with Erik watching over me.

Chapter 38: Nightmare

I can't breathe. My head is bleeding. What's going to happen to me? I'm going to die. I need to fight back, but he's just too strong.

"I've been waiting for this moment," he said cruelly.

I coughed up blood.

"I was hoping this wasn't going to be messy," he sighed, "you have to ruin everything don't you?"

I tried to get up but I couldn't. Where is Erik?

"You know what? I'll help you up. It will be more fun with you trying to get away. But you and I both know that's never going to happen," he said helping me to my feet.

I stood up fine considering that I could hardly breathe and my head was bleeding.

However, he was wrong. No matter how hurt or scared I was, I was not going down without a fight.

He lunged at me and I moved to the side.

"You're not going to fight now, are you? You can try but I'll still win. I always win."

Before I could react he pinned me down to the ground. I tried to get back up, but his grip was too strong.

"Oh Isabelle, you can't get away from me. Why bother trying?"

I spit blood in his face.

"Now that's just disgusting," he said wiping the blood off his face with his black leather glove. "You have absolutely no manners, do you?"

I tried kicking him off of me while he was distracted, but it didn't work. He pushed my head to the side, opened his mouth, and forced his teeth into my neck. It hurt like hell. I thought it was going to feel good because it always seems to in movies and books. Instead it was the worst pain I have ever endured. He wasn't trying to feed; he was trying to kill me! Blood was dripping everywhere from my neck.

"You taste delicious, but why don't I just put you out of your misery?" He said pulling a knife out of his pocket.

"Very original," were the last words I gasped.

"Goodnight," he whispered in my ear as he plunged the knife through my heart.

*

Uhhhhhh. I woke up screaming and holding my chest tight. It hurt. That wasn't just a dream, that was a vision. My dreams are never that vivid and I can never feel anything from them.

"Whoa, are you okay Iz?" James yelled running into my room. He had come in the morning to bring me breakfast or almost lunch because I slept so late.

"Yeah, just a bad dream as usual. How did you get in here?"

"I came in through the door; your mom didn't lock it when she left for the hospital. That's not a good thing to do with your killer on the loose."

"Oh, I thought you came through the window or something. I can't believe she didn't lock the door. What's a locked door gonna do anyway I guess, aren't vampires like super strong?"

"True, you're not safe either way. Erik and I decided that we'll have to have someone with you at all times."

"Like a supernatural bodyguard? I always wanted one of those," I joked.

James laughed, "Yes, exactly like that". He sat on my bed next to my feet. "Nice Mickey Mouse PJs."

"Really funny. I got them in Disney. Not that I don't love being with you, but why are you here?"

"Oh, because it's your birthday," he said wiggling my toes through my comforter.

"Did I seriously just forget that it's my birthday today?"

"Yes, yes you did. So, happy seventeenth birthday. That's one year older than you survived back then."

I guess he must really be giving me time. "Yeah, I guess it is." I gave James a half-happy smile.

"Oh, I almost forgot. Ready to go shopping?"

"For what?"

"Food for your party, and decorations. Now come on and get out of bed." He ripped the blankets right off me.

"But you, Erik, and Chris don't eat," I said lazily getting out of my bed.

"We don't, but you and your friends do. Don't you?"

"Yeah, we do, that's a silly question. What stores are we going to anyway?"

"Whatever ones you want to. Today is your day," James smiled. "Now hurry up!"

I looked at my dresser and there were flowers and balloons on it. There was a card with an iTunes gift card in it, too. It was weird reading 'love, mom' on the card with my dad's name missing.

"Okay, let's just go to the Party Superstore," I said not wanting to cry about my dad.

We got a bunch of stuff at the store including balloons and a banner that read: Happy 17th Birthday. I got a silly birthday crown and party hats for everyone. James didn't know my favorite foods anymore. I grabbed some bottles of Coke and Sprite. I also got my favorite sour cream and onion chips and crunchy nachos. James saw a bunch of pre-made wraps and sandwiches.

"You girls will eat this right?" He asked holding them up.

"Yeah, whatever is good but what about a cake?" I asked as we checked out of line.

"Got that covered, I picked it up earlier and it's in your freezer."

"What kind is it?"

"It's a Carvel ice-cream cake. I hope you like it. Now what are you going to wear Iz?"

"I love ice-cream cake! I think I'm just gonna wear...this," I laughed, pointing to the clothes I had on.

"You cannot wear that," James snickered. We walked to my car and James tossed the bags in the trunk.

"Then what do you suggest I wear?"

"You'll pick it out. I'll take you shopping. I'll drive to the mall." He got into the driver's seat of my car. So, I had to sit on the passenger's side.

"Whatever, can I get a bullet, knife proof jumpsuit in case my killer makes a surprise visit?"

"No, you won't need that. I'll get you something nice," James said rolling his eyes and speeding up the car.

We went to this pretty little dress shop called Moonlight Dancing. I tried on a bunch of dresses, but my mind was set on one. It was this cute black strapless dress with a violet satin belt going around the torso. The dress was a little bit above my knees. It was kind of pricey and I didn't want James to spend a lot of money on me.

"I don't know James; this dress is a lot of money."

"Iz, you look beautiful in it. Think of all the years that I haven't bought you a birthday present. Let me make up for it now."

"Okay, but only because you twisted my arm," I giggled and held the dress up to me.

"And why don't you get those black backless heels that I saw you eyeing in the window?"

"Okay, if you insist," I laughed.

As we made our way back to the car James said, "Well that worked out well. Now you don't have to wear shorts and a Hollister tank top to your party. What the hell…"

Suddenly a black Prius came flying up the parking lot. It zoomed right past us, so close to James it almost hit him.

"Get in the car now Iz," he screamed. "We're going after that idiot!"

"What, James no this is crazy," I said pulling at his arm.

He quickly pulled out of the spot and went right through the stop sign that led into the street.

I could see the Prius up ahead at the light, but there was so much traffic we couldn't get to it.

"Just forget it James we have to get back to my house and we are never going to catch up to him."

"Whatever, Iz but that person could give us a clue to whoever's after you."

He hit the gas anyway and cut off a couple of cars. I screamed for him to stop but he just wouldn't listen. After five blocks of trying to catch up to him, he pulled off onto a side street and we lost him. James looked pissed. He turned around fiercely and headed home.

Chapter 39: Party

Seven o'clock came quickly. By the time we got home and decorated I only had like ten minutes before my friends arrived.

"Well I'm going to go change," I said walking up the stairs.

"Okay, I'll set up the food, that's the one thing we didn't do," James said walking toward the kitchen.

I put on my new dress and shoes, and then started doing my hair. I curled it loosely, trying to make it look like my hair in my old life. I think I succeeded. After that I put my diamond stud earrings in.

"You look terrific," James said from the door.

"Thank you," I said turning to face him.

"But..." James trailed off.

Flashback

"But, what?"

"You're missing something," he said coming back in.

What am I missing? Other than a makeover? I have my outfit, my accessories and my makeup done.

"Missing what?"

"This," he said pulling something shiny out of his pocket and walking towards me.

"What is it?"

"You don't recognize it? I really thought you would have," he said putting it in my hair.

As soon as he did that, I knew what it was.

"My diamond hair clip!" I exclaimed. "You kept it all these years." I wrapped my arms around him excitedly.

"Yes, it was one of the only things father would let me keep of yours after you died."

"Oh, I am sorry," I sighed.

"Why are you sorry? You're here now aren't you?"

I felt tears welling up in my eyes. Actually having something from my past just reminded me even more of how much I missed it. A tear rolled down my cheek.

The doorbell rang. I let go of James and I ran down the stairs to open the door.

"Erik! I am so glad you came." I said hugging him tightly. I was just so happy to be spending my birthday with him, even with everything going on.

"Me too and you look beautiful." He kissed me right on my lips, so soft, so tender.

I melted. "Thanks."

"Am I interrupting something?" Chris asked walking up to the door. My stomach fluttered when I heard his voice.

"No, you're not." I said. I did not want to hurt his feelings.

Erik just stared at him.

"Are your friends here yet? I kind of like that Evelyn one. She reminds me of someone I used to know," Chris said.

"No, they're not here yet, but James is. He's upstairs if you want to go grab him."

I shut the door and Chris started up the stairs. The doorbell rang again. Sure enough it was Evelyn and Rachael. "Hey Iz," Rachael exclaimed coming in with her pink satin dress and bright pink high heels. Of course she's wearing that. She always had to look good, and of course she always does. She had hoop earrings and a Pandora bracelet on too.

"Happy Birthday Girl!" She giggled.

"Thank you!"

"Let's get this party started," Evelyn raised her arms and shouted, which made her blue ruffled dress with black belt go up to her butt. She too had matching heels.

We love our high heels. That's all we wanted for our birthdays when we were fifteen.

James came sliding down the banister. Chris followed.

"Good, your friends are here," they both said. We all just stood there crammed in the foyer.

"Who's the hottie?" Rachael asked.

"The hottie just so happens to be my brother," I blurted out without thinking.

"What? I thought you only have a sister," Rachael said.

"Just kidding. I mean he's like a brother to me. We met at camp years ago. But he moved to Connecticut," I said trying to cover it up.

"Good one," James muttered under his breath.

"Um, when did you ever go to camp?" Rachael laughed.

"I don't remember what year Rach, it was like forever ago," I brushed it off.

"Well let's not just stand here, let's go have some fun," Chris interrupted, and led us all into the living room.

Thank god he changed the subject. I don't know if they believed me or not.

"Thank you," I mouthed to Chris.

"Anytime," he mouthed back.

James turned on some music. He pushed the couches against the wall and moved my dad's recliner into the corner to make room for a dance floor. We were all dancing. I felt guilty about my sister not being there because she loves to dance. I can't believe my friends didn't think there is something up with Erik since he was dancing like it was the 19th century. I was about to grab his hand and join him in a two-step waltz.

"Time for presents," James said excited.

"I already gave her mine, let's see if anyone can top my awesome gift," Evelyn joked.

"Okay, who's going first?" James looked at Erik.

"I will," Chris volunteered. He handed me a little blue box with a bow wrapped around it.

I sat on my father's chair to open it.

"Go on open it," Chris urged me.

I opened the box and held up a crystal heart charm bracelet. "It's beautiful, is this real?"

"Yes, put it on," he said clasping the bracelet around my wrist.

I looked at Erik, he looked mad. "I'll give mine to you next," Erik said grinning.

Instead of handing me a box like Chris he told me to stand up and turn around. He took the present out of his pocket and put it around my neck. After he was done, I looked down and saw this gorgeous necklace. It was an amulet with a moon and a couple of diamonds around it. "I, I love it!"

"I am so glad, it was my mothers." He looked so happy that I loved it.

When he said that I remembered it was the same necklace he had given me in my old life. I couldn't believe he was able to get it after I passed away. My eyes filled with tears. I wanted to breakdown but I knew Rachael and Evelyn wouldn't understand. I held myself together.

"Thank you," I said kissing and hugging Erik. "You don't know how much this means to me."

"You're welcome and I do know what it means."

We held each other for a minute and I kind of forgot everyone else was there. Rachael and Evelyn just sat on the couch and stared at me. I am not usually so emotional in front of my friends and I thought I was doing a good job of not showing them.

"Okay, it's my turn now," James interrupted our hug and handed me a book.

"What is it?"

"Open it," he said eagerly.

So, I did. Inside there were photographs of me,

James, Daniel, and my father. They were so old. They look nothing like pictures do today. I remembered when the camera was first invented. Nathan's father had one at the ball. These pictures were from that night. This was by far the best present I have ever gotten. I couldn't believe he gave it to me in front of my friends. I didn't know what to tell them.

"Thank you James," I said getting all teary-eyed again.

My friends looked at me funny. "What are those old pictures?" Rachael asked.

"Pictures of my ancestors James dug up because his dad is a historian," I said. It was hard lying to my friends. I am not even sure half of my lies made sense. I wish I could just tell them everything. I know they would think I am nuts. They were already looking at me like I had two heads.

"You're welcome Iz."

"My turn, my turn," Rachael said way too overexcited. How much caffeine did she have today? I laughed.

"What, Isabelle?"

"Nothing." I said, holding my hand over my mouth.

"Oh, I forgot your present is in my car. I'll go get it," she said heading toward the door. "That's weird, the door is stuck or something."

Right after she said that, the lights went out. Someone screamed. The house seemed darker than usual and

Flashback

I could barely make out anyone in the room.

"Rachael," I shouted.

"I'm right here," she answered.

"Is everybody okay?" James shouted. "Everyone make your way toward the couch."

"Yes, but you aren't," someone said grabbing me.

I screamed. "Get off of me!"

"Leave her alone!" Erik shouted but it was too dark for me to see where he was.

James yelled, "Who the hell is touching my sister?"

"What's going on?" Rachael cried and somehow turned the lights back on.

I quickly kicked him in the shin, freed myself and ran towards Erik.

The man headed towards Rachael. He was wearing the same clothes he was wearing in the alley. His hoodie was so big you could hardly see his face.

"Calm down little girl, I'm not going to hurt you, just her." The man pointed to me, "and anyone who gets in my way." He then fiercely pushed Rachael to the ground and headed towards me. She looked hurt and kind of out of it.

"I won't let you hurt her," Evelyn screamed.

"What are you going to do about it, little protector? You may be strong for a little girl, but you aren't strong enough," he said looking at Evelyn.

Little protector? What the hell is he talking about? Is someone going to wake me up from this bad dream?

"She may not be strong enough, but she's not alone, she has us," Chris shouted.

We were all backed in the corner of the room. He was moving back and forth, to protect himself from every angle possible. He looked mad and strong, like a caged up tiger. I wasn't sure the guys could protect me from him.

"True, very true," the man said laughing as if he knew he could take us all down at once.

"Who are you?" I asked nervously. I was huddled up to Erik, too afraid to move.

"You already know. Think. Think hard." He grunted.

"Nathan? " I questioned. My voice quivered.

"No you idiot," he said pulling down his hood.

Daniel. It was Daniel. I don't know who was more surprised. James or me!

"No, no it couldn't be. I don't believe it. You couldn't have killed your own sister!" James screamed in disgust.

"Oh, but I did." He laughed.

"What, I don't understand this?" Rachael cried, looking scared and confused, shaking on the ground. Chris helped Rachael and pushed her towards the kitchen.

"It'll be okay Rachael. Evelyn, are you alright?" Chris asked.

"Yes, I'm not worried I already know everything," Evelyn said.

What? How does she know? Did my father know too? Is that why he sent someone a message that said contact Evelyn? I'll worry about that later if there is a later for me.

"But how could you bring yourself to hurt me Daniel? I loved you so much," I cried.

We were still in the corner of the room as Daniel came yelling towards us.

"You know what Erik did to me. That's why. He took away my life. I wanted to grow old and die with my wife. But I can't do that now. Plus, I always resented you for killing our mother."

"Isabelle did not kill our mother Daniel," James shouted.

"Yes she did, after Katherine was born mother became ill, and died. So now you will die again," he said as he lunged towards me, grabbing my neck, and throwing me down on the ground.

Erik tried to grab me but he was too quick for even him. Then Chris jumped in front of me and was thrown clear across the room knocking down every piece of furniture on the way.

Daniel leaped on top of me but Erik grasped the back of his shirt.

"No," he yelled and knocked him down beside me. Daniel's head bounced hard off of the ground temporarily stunning him.

"I, I can't breathe and my arm is bleeding." I screamed.

"Are you okay?" Erik asked me as he helped me to my feet.

I nodded.

"Watch out, he's getting up," Evelyn said as she jumped on Daniel's back, "Someone hand me something pointy."

James broke off a piece of wood from the table. All the food that was on it fell to the floor. He tossed the leg of the table to Evelyn.

"Got you," she said trying to stake Daniel, but he twisted her arm and then threw her over his head and smashed her hard onto the ground.

Erik lunged at him, but Daniel jumped to the side reaching for me. James blocked Daniel from grabbing me, and threw Daniel hard into the wall.

Daniel got back up quickly as James retrieved the

stake from Evelyn. James pinned Daniel to the wall. He thrust the stake into Daniel. The stake penetrated right above Daniel's heart.

"You wouldn't kill your own brother, would you?"

James hesitated.

"That's what I thought."

"Well you thought wrong Daniel," James said coldly, pushing harder on Daniel's neck.

"What?" Daniel acted surprised.

"If you could kill your own sister twice, I can kill my own brother," James said as he pulled out the stake from Daniel's cold body and re-staked Daniel through the heart.

In the middle of the living room Daniel burst into flames, and burned to ashes. The dust filled the room. It was surreal. My brother was now a pile of ashes. Daniel was really gone. I couldn't help but scream as water flooded my eyes. I collapsed on the ground.

"Iz, are you all right?" Erik asked cradling me in his arms.

"I..." I couldn't speak, I was in shock. My body trembled. My heart raced. Everyone hovered over me as I shook in Erik's arms.

"He was our brother Isabelle, that's why you're so upset, but it's for the best," James said kneeling down beside me and the ash pile of our brother.

"Is he dead?" Rachael asked as she slowly crept back into the room.

"He's dead, James killed him," Evelyn said.

"I'm sorry Isabelle, but now that he's gone, you can finally find out who you really are. You now have a chance to reach your full potential before they come for you," Chris said.

"Before who comes for me?" I looked up at him, even though my head was still spinning.

"You'll learn that in time, but what I would really like to know is why Daniel called Evelyn little protector?" Chris asked curiously.

"Yeah, why did he?" I asked.

Evelyn looked nervous. She kneeled down next to me and grabbed my hand. "Isabelle, I was your best friend, Lillian, back then, but I was also your protector. I reincarnated with you, I wish I could have told you sooner, but it was better you didn't know. Chris is right, you are special. They will come for you. It's my job to protect you Isabelle, always."

We all just sat there speechless. I just wanted my 17th birthday to be over.

To be continued...

Flashback

Made in the USA
Charleston, SC
13 June 2012